SNAP

NEW TALENT

THE KANDESKY VAMPIRE CHRONICLES BOOK TWO

MICHELE DRIER

SNAP: New Talent
Copyright 2012 Michele Drier. All Rights Reserved
Published by Michele Drier

ISBN: 978-1479366453

Cover by Jenny Rosenberg
Typesetting by jimandzetta.com

Books by Michele Drier

The Kandesky Vampire Chronicles
Book One, SNAP: The World Unfolds
Book Two, SNAP: New Talent
Book Three, Plague: A Love Story

The Amy Hobbes series
Edited for Death

In the second book of the SNAP Kandesky vampire series, Maxie Gwenoch, media-savvy editor of the multinational celeb gossip magazine SNAP, is pummeled in Paris and kidnapped in Kiev as the Huszars ramp up the race to oust their centuries-old rivals, the Kandeskys.

SNAP's owners, the Kandesky family of vampires, built the world's most popular celeb coverage empire but this isn't just a business take-over. These powerful vampire families lived with an uneasy peace for four centuries until Maxie came in to boost SNAP's coverage and started making inroads into the Huszar's traditional hunting territories.

Although Jean-Louis, Maxie's lover, vampire and second-in-command of the Kandeskys, tries to keep her safe, Maxie is determined to do things her way, a way that may lose her her job, her love and her life.

For Darcy, Matt and the girls

SNAP
New Talent

Copyright 2012 by Michele Drier

Acknowledgements

First, to all those people who live in my head: my mother, who daily watches me from the top of the Montmartre Steps, my grandmother, who sits on several bookcases and my great-great-grandmother whose ring I wear. You are forever a part of me, and I'm glad.

Also, Darcy, Illa and Susan who have listened to me, my critique partners at the Capitol Crimes Chapter of Sisters in Crime, beta readers Sharon Cronin and Jackie Timmons and to my first, last and best critic and fan, Beth White. We'll get that shelf of books, yet!

This is a work of fiction.

Chapter One

Every time I slept, I dreamt.

These weren't everyday dreams though. My subconscious fears grabbed hold of me and dragged me into a world of noise and fury that only stopped when I forced myself awake. Then the sounds of leathery wings and scratching, small talons faded.

This time I woke up because Elise was in the room, moving the drapes aside to a pale day.

"Good day," she looked at me. "Did you, were you dreaming again?"

I pulled myself up in bed, saw that the sun was at a low angle trying to get through a gray mist. "What time is it?"

"Just before 3," Elise called from the small kitchen area. I smelled fresh coffee, then she carried a tray of coffee server, cup, two fresh rolls, butter and jam to the round table set before the windows. I pulled on a long sweatshirt from the bottom of the bed and headed into the bathroom.

I was still uncomfortable sharing my living space with another person, especially a maid. Coming from the classless United States and L.A. ,the capital of laid-back, I had to remember not to be so casual as to wear only a tee shirt but I discovered that a long zip sweatshirt was comfortable and could pass for a robe just between Elise and me.

"Do you want to have coffee before your shower? What will you being doing today?" Elise's questions weren't nosy, she was trying to find out what clothes I'd need for the coming day and night.

With coffee in front of me, I was able to banish the last of the wings and claws. "Today is primarily a work day." I broke off a chunk of the roll, smeared it with butter and added a spoonful of jam. "I think just wool slacks and a sweater. If I go out, it will only be for a short walk and I can grab a jacket and some boots from the armory."

Elise nodded as she went into the closet to find and lay out clothes. "Will it just be us for dinner?"

I glanced up sharply. Was she trying to pry? Did I sense some disapproval in her tone? Her back was to me, but when she turned around with slacks and a sweater draped over her arm, her faced was placid. Was I ever going to be able to understand the subtext of these Europeans? Or was there even a subtext? Was I reading too much, or maybe too little, into their language?

My only language was English, and I thought I understood nuances, but I was surrounded by people who spoke several languages—Hungarian, German, French. Spanish, Portuguese, and now Polish, Czech and Russian—in addition to English. Some of them spoke several of the languages, but all of them spoke English and Hungarian. What they spoke, though, may have been different from what they said and what they meant.

It wasn't worth going into with Elise. She was always polite, always helpful, and tried to fit herself around my needs and wants. If she did disapprove of anything I did, she knew it wasn't her place to note it or voice it and I respected her circumspection. I never felt the stink-eye from any of the other house staff, so either Elise never talked, or everyone was too well-trained to let on.

Today was going to be a work day. Getting started in the afternoon wasn't as slothful as it sounded. My employer, Baron Stefan Kandesky, and his family, own the multi-national, multi-media conglomerate, SNAP.

SNAP produced celebrity news and gossip 24/7 through television and weekly magazines that came out in zoned editions, and languages, in the United States, Britain, France, Germany (and German speaking countries), Brazil,

Spain, Australia and New Zealand. Covering most of the world meant that at any given time somebody was at work in the many offices, so my 12-hour days could start and finish any time. Besides, starting work in the late afternoon also gave me the night hours to interact with my bosses, all members of the Kandesky family—a family of Hungarian vampires.

Chapter Two

Checking email was always top priority. When I took the job with SNAP, I was the Managing Editor of the weekly magazine and worked in the headquarter Los Angeles offices. SNAP may be a multi-national business, but its primary business was celeb gossip and coverage, and the firmament of stars that people want to hear about intersects with SoCal.

Jasmine Fall, Just-Call-Me-Jazz, initially my assistant, was now holding down the L.A. office. We communicated a couple of times a day by phone; once by Skype for the daily content meeting, with senior eds, art people and TV producers, and constantly by email. If it needed immediate attention, I was called, but Jazz was getting very proficient at sorting through the "I have to speak with her" from the "I know she'll take my call".

Only drawback was that my commute time now didn't give me time to get into work mode. In L.A., I always used the commute, usually in a town car, to make lists. Lists of what I had to do at home and then the transition to lists of work-related chores. I also scanned the Los Angeles and New York *Times*. Depending on traffic, it was around 30 minutes from my condo in Santa Monica and I could hit the elevators at a run.

Now, I walked across my suite to my office, a distance of less than 50 feet. Not enough time to wake up if I hadn't had coffee.

Today's—actually last night's in West Coast time—spate of emails was the usual. Notes about people to see, an update of my travel calendar, a nice gossipy one about office politics, romances and spats. I answered the ones that needed it, stuck some in folders and deleted a lot. Despite both Jazz' and my foot-stomping, there were always some people who could and would sneak a cc or a "reply to all" in.

It would be a few more hours before I could talk to anybody on the Coast, so I started on European calls.

"'Allo, Maxie," François' cheery voice lightened my day. "I don't have much for you. When are you coming to see me?"

François headed the Paris office, although he spent time in L.A. as well. He was young, hip, cutting-edge and irreverent and we had fun together.

"Next week for a few days if I can clear some other things up. I need to get to Prague, too, and was hoping you'd go with."

"Hummmm..." I could practically hear the gears ticking over. "I can manage maybe three days after next week?"

"That would be great!" My enthusiasm wasn't faked, Francois made a good traveling pal. Like the rest of the Kandesky family, he knew Europe well. After all, he'd lived here for more than 300 years.

When I took the job with SNAP, I was stunned at the perks and goodies that came with being in upper management. For the first time in my life, I could use personal shoppers. I had decorators when I needed them. There were limos, caterers, best tables at restaurants and people actually returned my calls.

There were also body guards and personal planes and being watched 24/7. It was like a prison, but gilded with the best.

The Kandesky family, named for their head, Baron Stefan Kandesky, was large, incredibly wealthy, urbane, mannered and constantly on guard with their archrivals, another Central European vampire family, the Huszars. This feud dated back about 500 years so the Kandeskys had plenty of time to figure out protection strategies.

The further I became enmeshed in the family and in SNAP, the more I learned what my value was. And as I began to fall in love with Jean Louis, titular art director for SNAP the

Magazine and second-in-command of the Kandesky family, I felt as though they were staking me out as tiger bait for the Huszars.

I fought against it, fought with Jean Louis, but if I wanted to keep my job and wanted to stay close to this stunning man—who happened to be a several-centuries-old vampire—I had to listen and obey.

Which is how I ended up living in a castle in Hungary, with a live-in maid, hot and cold running demons to guard me, and shopping trips to Paris.

And, oh yes, Jean Louis, on occasion.

San Quentin it wasn't.

Chapter Three

I suppose I could have just let SNAP and all it meant to me go, but I wasn't raised that way. I'd worked hard to get to where I was. As much as I wanted Jean Louis, and as much as I loved the luxe life I was leading, my soul needed to know that I had value beyond my personal life.

There are probably those who believe that media like SNAP are parasites and not really journalism, and they may be right. I've never viewed my career in celeb gossip as earth-shaking, but it provides everybody a chance to see celebrities—movie stars, aristocrats, athletes, rock stars, the rich and beautiful—in an up-close-and-personal way.

The bottom line is that people are curious, they want to see what that singer who makes $15 million a year really eats, how she dresses when she takes a walk with her kids. And one of the first rules I'd laid down was that we would not buy any pictures from paparazzi who pushed the envelop. If one celebrity complained about being harassed, that photographer was banned from SNAP for life. A big blow for people who made a living following celebs, because we paid well and bought a lot of art.

And one of Jazz' emails brought that home. A wealthy gem trader in Sao Paulo complained that a young and hungry photographer bribed his gate guard, got on the grounds of his estate and shot pictures of his daughter's bedroom with a long lens. The guard was fired; Mira, our Senior Editor for the Brazilian office, fired the photographer, sent messages to all the other gossip channels and that guy was toast. Jazz made sure that I was cc'ed on the email chain.

By 5 p.m. I'd dealt with the routine stuff and needed to

get some fresh air. When I opened the door to my suite, the guard demon loomed in front of me.

"Can I help you with something?"

This was someone new. "Who are you? Where's my regular guard?"

He nodded in recognition that I'd asked a question, but he didn't smile. The demons seldom smiled, even though I tried my best to crack jokes with them. I'd gotten to know the chief demon, or head demon, or demon-manager (I still don't have their organizational chart memorized) Sandor well enough that he sometimes unbent and smiled, but the minions weren't amused. Kind of like talking to the Coldstream Guards at the Tower of London.

"I have no information. Sandor told me to take the day shift at your door." The demon was dressed in the ubiquitous black suit, well-enough cut to camouflage the Sig Sauer in the shoulder holster, and starched white shirt.

"I'm going out to take a walk before it gets any darker." I was pulling on my jacket as I came into the hall. "Are you the one assigned to stay with me?"

A slight nod said yes as he poured a rapid burst of Hungarian into his communicator. Whoever was on the other end must have agreed, because he nodded again and turned to me. "We go now," he waved me down the hall toward the stairs.

Outside, the October day was fading fast, but there was still enough light that the hardwood trees flamed against the darkening sky. Coming from SoCal, the actual change in season was amazing to me. Not that there weren't seasons in California, there were. Fall was fire season, when the Santa Ana winds came off the desert and dried the brush-covered hills to tinder and late winter, usually February, was the warm season with clear, balmy days. This was when the local Chambers of Commerce took their promo pictures, before the inland valleys heated up and sucked fog off the ocean. Then came smog season for a few months, before the Santa Anas came around again.

But fall here in the foothills of the Carpathians was an honest season. The air had a snap and tang to it, the nights cooling, the trees turning color and dropping their leaves. And the feral pigs of the Huszars beginning to run on their truffle hunts. I'd learned my lesson during the summer and didn't walk into the woods or to the fishing steam after dark, when other hangers-on of the Huszars were out on their guarding and hunting forays.

With a demon though, I was safe enough to walk the edges of the Baron's property and even as far as the trout stream while it was still light. Today, the mist had cleared and the air was so crisp that I could taste it with every breath. We— I'd have to ask Sandor the demon's name, I hated just saying "hey, you"—followed the cleared path to the stream.

During the spring and summer, when the Baron had regulars from the media and film industries as guests at the castle, there was practically a traffic jam on this path. This part of the mountains, and a big part of Slovenia, were famous for their crystal-clear trout streams and lured anglers from around the world. The locals played it cagey. An angler had to have a local license, sold by the area, and it was only for catch-and-release, so a lot of big fish made it into digital albums but not onto dinner plates or wall plaques.

I wasn't interested in the fishing. This was a small, cold stream that reminded me of the Merced River coming out of Yosemite. My family took a couple of vacations there when I was a kid, and now this took me back to a time of safety, with no worries.

Was I safe now?

Chapter Four

Dark was coming up fast when the unnamed demon and I came into the castle's armory. Sandor was in there, cleaning and oiling guns and he looked up and nodded as the door closed behind us.

"There you are Maxie. Did you and Vladmir see anything of interest outside?"

Ah ha, Vladmir. Good to know his name, but all the demons were large and all dressed in black suits. As hard as they were to tell apart, I wasn't sure most regulars bothered to find out their names. As for the others, well the staff saw them every day and the vampires had known them for centuries, so no wonder they didn't bother to introduce themselves.

Vladmir let loose with a long string of words in a language I not only didn't know but couldn't even place. My jaw must have been hanging, because Sandor turned to me. "Vladmir is speaking Russian. I'm assigning him as part of your guard contingent because of your new coverage."

What new coverage? What the hell did the demon-in-chief know about my job that I didn't know? Once again, I was getting the run-around and it steamed me.

I opened my mouth to make a snarky comment, but Sandor powered on again in Russian then turned to me. "Vladmir says that he sensed some unease in the Neutrality. Nothing specific, but he also heard the feral pigs. Did you hear them?"

"No, but I can never hear anything over the stream noise. What do you mean about my new area?"

His communicator buzzed, a quick burst of Hungarian

and he said, "That was Elise looking for you. She needs you to get ready for dinner."

"Humph..." was as much as I could muster. It wouldn't do to have an unamiable conversation with a demon, and for sure not in front of one of his staff, or whatever they were called.

Pulling myself up to my full 5 foot 8 inches, I snapped my head around and headed to my suite. Dressing for dinner now, unless Elise and I were just eating in my suite, didn't just mean taking off jammies and putting on jeans.

The Kandeskys and their formal European ways were starting to rub off my sharp edges. First was the dress. They weren't stodgy, but casual meant a pair of fine wool slacks and a cashmere sweater or a simple silk and wool dress. This was appropriate for wear around the house, a walk or a quick trip into the closest village. Beyond that, the sweater was accessorized, a matching jacket and heels were added, or a daytime suit was in order.

And for a "family" dinner, meaning whoever was currently living in or visiting the castle, dresses were in order—simple cocktail or plain dinner dresses. When guests were entertained, three or four times a month, it was true dinner dressing. Long dresses for the women, dinner suits for the men, who could sometimes get by with a good black suit, white shirt and tasteful tie.

It was fun for somebody who loved playing dress-up as a kid, but I also found out it was time-consuming. It meant at least two changes of clothes during a day and at least one redo of hair and makeup. How anyone managed this without a maid, I didn't know. Elise kept track of my clothes, laid out what I needed and took care of all the little details like ordering soap and cosmetics. My suite was always immaculate, I never ran out of coffee or shampoo or toilet paper, like in the good old days. I didn't even have to keep a shopping list.

The wardrobe I'd brought from L.A. wasn't up to this, either in quantity or quality. Thank God Jazz had set me up with a couple of personal shoppers before my first trip to Hungary, so I had some basics and she'd overnight me things every so often.

This was another reason for my few days in Paris with François. Most of the Kandeskys—certainly the women—shopped in Paris a few times a year and watched the spring and fall shows. When I was moving to the castle, and leaving all that was familiar behind me, Jean-Louis laughed as I was deciding what to take and packing.

"You're going to be staying at Stefan's castle. There are servants. You have a suite of rooms assigned to you. You're in Europe. You can have the plane, or the demons, take you to Rome, Milan, Paris. If you truly run out of something from here, you can have me or Carola or Mira pick it up on one of our trips. You can call Jazz and have her send it!" and then accused me of acting as though I was going into exile.

It sure hadn't been exile; if anything I felt too accessible at times. Life wasn't just changing clothes and shopping, I was getting work done but still wasn't sure of the best direction for expansion. My title was International Planning Editor, a title the vampires had dreamed up when my presence in L.A. was getting too close to the Huszars for comfort.

I initially thought it was just an empty title and I'd continue as Managing Editor for SNAP, The Magazine, working remotely. Wrong.

The Kandeskys hadn't cornered the market on the world's celeb gossip by willy-nilly handing out titles and huge salaries for nothing. Several hours every day were spent in reading (translated of course, I still hadn't learned any other languages and didn't think I'd ever have the time) newspapers, magazines, faxes and emails from countries in the former Eastern Bloc.

SNAP was paying for sources to provide names, tips and gossip about anybody they deemed "interesting". It was my job to try and sort this volume of information into some sensible package that would translate to magazine editions and I was still on the first task: identifying the correct movers and shakers in Poland, Ukraine and Russia, with a few from the Baltic states thrown in for good measure.

Language was going to be the biggest decider for new editions. I figured we'd add Polish and Russian, but our circulation wouldn't support an edition in Lithuanian or Estonian. Those countries would receive the nightly TV show with sub-titles and voice-over translations.

This suddenly brought me smack up to Vladmir, again. Sandor said "for my new assignment." Was I getting sent to Russia? Moscow? Oh Lord, I couldn't manage that.

I practically stomped up the last set of stairs to my suite, building up a head of steam. Elise took one look at me. "I laid out your Dolce & Gabbana dress, but I think I'll change it to a black Chanel suit." She picked up a filmy armful of silk chiffon, headed for the dressing room and came back with a flared skirt, cropped jacket suit and a white, drapy silk shell. "I think just pearls and some gold bangles. "

She was too well-trained and well-mannered to ask me directly what was wrong, but she sure sensed something was. I knew she'd have a talk with some of the other servants later and among them they might be able to figure out my snit.

As I was putting the pearls in my ears, already dressed, hair done and make-up on, there was a tapping at the front door. I caught a glimpse of Elise's face in the mirror and nodded to let him in.

Jean-Louis looked good, really good, tonight. I suspected he'd taken care to look good because he was going to sell me on something, again, that I wouldn't want.

"You look business-like, tonight, love." Aha! Something was afoot. He called me "Max", or "My Dear" as a rule, "love" was reserved for special occasions and this wasn't one of *those* special occasions.

"Thank you. I thought after we watch the live feed, we could talk about the best direction to head in the east. Did you have something planned?"

Hah, one of the things I'd learned early on was the use of a passive-aggressive offense, which usually worked well if I didn't have all the information. Because of Sandor's comment about my new assignment, I knew Jean-Louis and the Baron had something planned for me. My little comment meant that now he was going to have to come clean about some of the plans, although it would take more probing to get the whole scoop.

Chapter Five

Jean-Louis gave me a long, speculative look. "Stefan and I are planning to meet with some of the Huszars this evening, but I can carve out some time to talk to you."

Damn the man. It would be a lot easier for me to stand my ground if he weren't so...so...

He suddenly grinned, a smile so broad it crinkled the corners of his eyes and showed the tips of his fangs. "You were going to say 'attractive'?"

"I wish you wouldn't do that! I hate it when you can read my mind."

His grin stayed. "I've told you, I, we, can't read minds. But after several centuries of interacting with regulars, we have body language down pat. You're just too transparent."

"I may be transparent, but I'm pretty miffed. Once again, I find out from the help that you have plans for me...this time the demons! Why can't you just talk to me first?"

Now his grin was fading, but he was beginning to glimmer, a sure sign he was planning to coerce me in other ways.

"Of course I was, I am, going to talk to you. I wanted to get a time when I could explain the whole plan, a time when we wouldn't be interrupted. You have to admit that, even though you're doing a great job of trying to adjust to our schedule, there's not always a lot of time together."

He was right, as usual. He and the other vampires had some flexibility even in daylight if they stayed indoors or traveled in their limos with heavily tinted windows. But they did most of their business and socializing at night, which meant that my sleep patterns were the ones that got adjusted. Also, the fact that I had to be awake during the day to do business when I traveled disrupted my schedule.

"Well, I'm awake now—I slept late this afternoon—so I have time tonight for a discussion." I knew my tone was waspish but I couldn't stop.

"We need to go down to dinner now, you know how Stefan is about punctuality." Jean-Louis' glimmer was deepening. "But I promise you, after the daily, we'll spend time and I'll fill you in."

This was as good as I was going to get. I tried to get rid of my frown but couldn't make it to a smile. "I'm looking forward to it," I said as I sailed out the door, almost tripping over Vladmir on the way.

Jean-Louis was tuned into my mood. He didn't even snicker, just caught up with me, took my arm and guided me to the stairs. "I should tell you, we have two of the young Huszars with us for dinner tonight."

I stopped so fast that he stepped on my toe. "Ow, get off of me," I hissed. "Why didn't you tell me?"

He took a half step backwards, and off the toe of my Christian Loubautin pump.

"Just when would you have liked me to tell you? At 6 this morning when we invited them? I know how you love to be waked up. Or, I could have sent you a message with Vladmir, you're so polite when staff members know something you don't. Or maybe I could have written you a note, or sent you an email...you'd have loved the personal touch in that."

Whoa, he may have stepped on my toe but I stomped all over his ego.

"Ok, ok, our schedules just aren't meshing. Which Huszars are coming?"

"Alessandr and Markov."

"I've met Alessandr, but who is Markov? That doesn't seem like a Hungarian name." I was speaking quietly. It wouldn't do to have Vladmir hear our little spat. He may not speak English, but he could sure pick up on tone.

"Just like us, not all of the Huszars are Hungarian. Markov is an ethnic Ukrainian whose name was Russianized during the Soviet era. He lives outside of Kiev when he's not here. Karoly and Alessandr are working with him."

Since moving to the castle, I was learning more than I wanted to know about the relations between the Kandeskys and the Huszars. The last two great vampire families in Middle Europe, they'd been at odds with one another for centuries.

The patriarchs of the families, Stefan Kandesky and Felix Huszar, had both been turned in the 15th century, but by different earlier vampires who were living in the forests, feeding off villagers.

Over the succeeding centuries, the families took different paths. Stefan fell in love with the daughter of a minor noble, turned her and took her father's title of Baron when the old man died, unaware that his daughter now had eternal life. They gathered others, expanded their range into neighboring countries, took acolytes and realized that making money was a better survival tool than murder. And, you didn't get chased, you got honored.

By the early 20th century, the Kandeskys were living across Europe, making millions every year from trade. They watched the rise of the entertainment industry, realized that it was almost as lucrative as minting money, and moved into the United States, cornering a chunk of the early movie fan market. When entertainment took off and spread, so did the Kandeskys until they now held the top spot in celebrity news and gossip across Europe and the Western Hemisphere.

The Huszars were homebodies. They stayed in Middle Europe, didn't take acolytes, hunted for their food and generally made themselves a scourge of the country-side. After 400 years, they'd eliminated the smaller vampire families, as well as the residents of several villages, and were being forced to hunt further afield.

Although they didn't need money to feed themselves, they did need it to keep up their living areas. There were repairs to the castles and outbuildings, money to bring in electricity and indoor plumbing, money for transportation. The Huszars earned this by hunting, cultivating and harvesting truffles. Teaming up with werewolves, they followed the feral pigs of the forests, eventually using them for hunting prey as well as truffles in the oak forests. They used servants, who lived the life of feudal serfs, to gather, pack and sell the truffles throughout Europe, and when the serfs outlived their usefulness, they became a meal.

Felix Huszar ruled his family with an iron hand for more than 300 years, only making one mistake. He adopted a young, beautiful man from a tiny village without a name in a country that became Bulgaria. No one remembered or cared where Matthais came from, and they learned not to ask.

Within a few years of becoming a Huszar, Matthais had gathered a following among the younger and newer family members. They were tired of living in the 15th century and watched their neighbors, the Kandeskys, as they took on the trappings of the uber-wealthy of the 20th century.

The Baron and his family traveled the world, and in style. They had planes, limos, yachts, lovely women and power. Politicians, movie stars, sports stars, just plain rich celebrities, courted them. No one turned down an invitation to a party, especially one at the Baron's castle.

During the Kandesky's rise, Matthais watched. What good was eternal life if every day was just like the one before, and would be just the same the day after?

When Felix' decaying body was found along a path in the Neutrality, and Matthais took the reins of the family, the feud that had simmered for centuries burst into flame. Matthais accused Kandeskys of murdering Felix to gain control of the Neutrality. Stefan and Felix had carved out the Neutrality on the border between their territories years before. Patrolled by Huszar werewolves and Kandesky demons, the area buffered the violence and became the place where the families could come together in relative peace...at least they wouldn't be killed while there.

With a new head of the Huszar family, the ancient pact seemed doomed. Matthais sent teams of werewolves and shapeshifters into the Neutrality, setting traps for anyone who came through. And when a Kandesky was caught, he was dragged in front of Matthais who was willing to ransom him back to the Kandeskys.

I knew this had been the state of the relationship between the families, but it changed when I came into the picture.

Baron Stefan Kandesky hired me to take over the print side of the SNAP empire, the weekly celebrity magazine with editions in English, German, French, Portuguese and Spanish. My job was to bolster circulation while researching and developing new markets. And those new markets were where? In the former Eastern Bloc and Soviet middle Europe. The area that the Huszars thought of as theirs.

So now the Kandeskys were poaching on Huszar territories, and doing it in a way that would make them even more money. Matthais was livid.

And because I was the agent that would make all this happen for the Kandeskys, I was the bulls-eye for Matthais' rage.

With that, I came down the stairs to have dinner with emissaries from the Huszars. Why should I be upset?

Chapter Six

There were eight of us for dinner. Penelope, the Baron's partner, and I were the only women. And I was the only regular. While I ate trout from the river, a rack of lamb and profiteroles for dessert, they had a dark-red consommé, steak tartare without the egg and blood pudding. I was getting used to mealtime and I knew the household staff, regulars all, were eating the same menu I ate, so I'd gotten over my guilt for making the cooks work so hard at fixing different food.

Alessandr was as I remembered him, polite with late 19th century Viennese manners. He took my hand to his lips and said quietly, "Mlle. Maxie, it is a pleasure, as always, to see you. May I introduce my colleague, Markov."

I wasn't sure the rough edges would ever get rubbed off of My-colleague-Markov. Because it was the Baron's dining room, I extended my hand and found it crushed in what I could only call a paw.

Markov was shorter than I and built like a gym rat on steroids. He was dark, with black eyes and black hair extending to the backs of his hands and fingers. His neck was as wide as his head, his shoulders made his dark suit look painted on and his arms were so muscled they angled out from his body.

"I'm happy to meet you," finally came out of my mouth as I tried not to snatch my hand back.

"I've heard much about you," Markov rumbled from somewhere in his chest. "I can see that Alessandr didn't exaggerate your beauty."

I began to wonder if the young Huszars had brought in a ringer, one of their werewolves, to case the castle and assess the Kandesky power, but Jean-Louis took my arm again and led me to a seat while chattering on to Markov in some language I didn't recognize. When we were seated, he turned to me. "Markov is from the former USSR, actually Ukraine. It's so difficult to keep all these silly political divisions straight. This part of Central Europe has changed names and allegiances so much over the years that I'm surprised the languages are still being spoken."

I looked at Jean-Louis. His glimmer was increasing and his eyes held the message "don't ask me any questions right now". Well, okay, I was too spooked to even figure out a question to ask. He'd told me enough about Markov that I was warned. Markov predated the Soviet era, but how far back he went I had no idea and his politics were unknown.

Dinner passed uneventfully. Most of the conversation was in Hungarian and what I was now recognizing as Russian. Jean-Louis leaned over a couple of times to translate a remark for me, but the context seemed to be the difference in the East bloc since the USSR collapsed. Much of the Soviet-styled building that happened after WWII was being demolished and cities were beginning to have an overlay of modern glass skyscrapers abutting 18th and 19th century municipal offices. Marble and stone, blackened by years of coal smoke and left to squalor in the Soviet era were being steam-cleaned and the result was a whiteness that hurt the eyes.

This was all very interesting, but didn't have any bearing on why the Huszars were here and what they were going to meet about later.

The Baron finally stood. "I think we'll have our coffee in the screening room and tonight we have a special treat for Maxie." He raised his wine glass, with a trace of the Bull's Blood they all drank, lying pinkish in the bottom. I raised my eyebrows and Jean-Louis raised his glass to me. "We're watching last night's U.S. show on tape delay."

This was a change. We usually watched one of the European versions, with only an hour or two difference.

"Thank you. Why are you doing this?" These vampires

didn't just go out of their way, or change their customs, on a whim.

"We thought Alessandr and Markov should see a U.S. version. This is where we started and it's still the version that's seen by most people around the world. And it's the model for all the other versions." With that, Stefan held out his arm for Penelope, Jean-Louis rose and gave me his hand and we led Milos and Bela the other two Kandeskys, along with the two Huszars, into the screening room.

Coffee and tea had already been set up on the side buffet. We chose places and settled in to watch last night's episode of "SNAP". The music came up and the anchor, a young, blond woman whom Jazz detested, welcomed viewers in a perky voice. I slid my eyes to Alessandr and Markov. They were fixated on the blond, but I wasn't sure if it was her pale skin or tight dress that attracted them most. They might be vampires, but they were also guys.

When it was over, there was a babble of Russian and Hungarian as they shifted their chairs to gather around a small conference table. I raised my eyebrows at Jean-Louis and he turned to Stefan.

"I need to talk to Maxie for a minute, first. Start without me and I'll catch up," he said in English, then added a sentence in Hungarian that caused Stefan to purse his lips.

Now what? Did the Baron regard me as a pain-in-the-ass hanger-on? I knew the Huszars were interested in me. They had, in fact, tried to kidnap me a few times, which is how I ended up living at the castle with round-the-clock demons watching me. Was something new happening? Had I shifted from the whiz-bang guru of the print product to "Oh, that's Jean-Louis' new fling?"

I stalked out of the screening room ahead of Jean-Louis and turned toward the library, half hoping he wouldn't follow. That would give me a lot of psychic chips to use in this game, but he was right there, reaching over to open the door for me.

I moved over to a couch in front of the long windows,

which now only reflected the warm room against the deep black velvet of a moonless Hungarian night. He took a chair beside me. Hmmm. In our little one-ups-man-ship game, did that signify?

"We need to clear the air, again." His voice sounded, what—tired, peeved, indifferent? When I glanced over, the glimmer had faded, not a good sign.

"Something happened today that set you off. What was it?"

"I took a walk down to the river this afternoon and when Vladmir and I came back through the armory, Sandor said that Vladmir had been assigned to me because of what I was going to do next. That meant that Sandor, and probably Vladmir, whom I'd never met before, both knew what I was about to do, where I was about to go, before I did. And that made me feel like chopped liver."

"'Chopped liver'? What the hell does that have to do with anything." Jean-Louis was honestly stumped, enough so that he wasn't furious.

"It's just an expression. It means, well, that something's not good enough. Instead of being a fancy pate de fois gras, you're only chopped liver." Explaining it like that made me feel pretty petty and using an American colloquialism was something I tried not to do, because it always threw the vampires who spoke the classical and upper-class dialects of the languages.

Watching me stumble around trying to make sense of chopped liver, watching my face start to get pink, Jean-Louis lost some of his anger.

"We do have differences. You're right, I don't always tell you everything, but that's because I'm not used to caring about someone, or having someone in my world who cares about me. My focus has been the family and the business, so my confidants have been Stefan, sometimes Milos and Bela from the village here, occasionally Pen and the SNAP executive team."

That was a long statement, and one probably hard for

him to make. He was this stunning man, at ease anywhere in the world, speaking several languages, able to hold his own against the best art directors in the business. And he's apologizing to me. Well, he didn't say "I'm sorry," but this was the closest I'd ever get to it and it popped my bubble of anger.

"I don't like that I get so hurt by you." I got up and moved to the arm of his chair. "I'm like you, I just haven't had anybody to care about for so long, that I've woven a little world of my own and I'm the king, or queen...the most important person, anyway, and don't have to answer to anybody. I'm used to being in a world where people worry about my moods, not where I have worry about some one else's. Wow, when two egoists like us come together, there's liable to be collateral damage!"

He reached up and stroked my face, following the line on my chin with one of his long, sensuous fingers. I slid into his lap and nestled my head into his shoulder.

"If you keep trying to remember to tell me things, to take me into your confidence, to let me help you plan, I will try not to take everything as a personal slight."

He nodded so I said, "Now, what plans do you have for me that the demons already know about?"

Chapter Seven

Jean-Louis moved so suddenly I almost landed on the floor. "My God, woman, you just never give up! You know that we've been talking about opening new outlets in the east...Ukraine, Russia, why is this such a big surprise?"

Hah, I was right! I *was* getting shipped to Moscow!

"When do I have to leave?" The thought of going to a strange city, a cold place where I knew no one and didn't speak—or for that matter, read—the language, with only Vladmir for companionship and safety made chills run down my spine. Jean-Louis wouldn't subject me to a long absence, would he?

"Leave? Where are you going?" I would swear his puzzled look was real.

"You're sending me to Russia, to Moscow, aren't you?"

This time I did end up on the floor as this beautiful vampire threw back his head and laughed so hard he convulsed.

"Where do you come up with these...these...ideas? Who ever said you were going to Moscow?"

"Well, there's Vladmir, there's everybody suddenly speaking Russian. And what about Markov at dinner?" My indignation was tempered with my being on the floor in a Chanel suit with a skirt so tight I couldn't bend a knee.

Jean-Louis' laughter tapered off, he stood up, lifted me to my feet and wrapped his arms around me. "I swear, you don't rush to these weird assumptions when you're making business decisions. What makes you do it where I'm concerned?"

He brought me up short. I didn't make half-assed assumptions in business. I asked questions, researched, knew all the information before I decided. That I did it so fast, and accurately, was what made me valuable; so valuable that SNAP hired me and the Huszars wanted me. When I came to my personal life, my life with Jean-Louis, well, if there was a dead-end road available, I took it.

"It's because of you. I've never felt like this before. I've never met anyone like you before."

"You mean because I'm a vampire? And I'm, oh, about 450 years older than you? And we have just slightly more money than Bill Gates... or the Habsburgs used to?"

"Well, there's all of that. But I think it's an emotional vulnerability. It's frightening to me to realize that I'm in love with you. Before, if I could keep it casual, if I could keep my own life away, inside myself, it didn't matter so much if it wasn't reciprocated, if the man moved on. Now, I'm terrified that I'll lose you, or you'll tire of me."

He put his finger across my lips, until I stopped talking and then kissed me, deeply and carefully, making the long bones in my legs melt.

"And how do you think I feel, knowing that you'll age and I won't? That eventually you'll die and leave me? That's one reason Pen and Stefan are worried about us, about me. They watched me go though several affairs with regulars after Magda was killed and all that emotional upheaval pulled me away from SNAP and away from the family. I'm second in command of the family, and there are a lot of very old souls who rely on me, for whom I'm responsible."

And here was where so many of our arguments started.

As the second in the family, it was up to Jean-Louis to watch the Huszars, to track their movements and to anticipate their changes. For a long while, this meant working with the demons, watching the Neutrality, keeping tabs on deaths and disappearances in the Carpathians and the surrounding areas.

But when SNAP built a 24/7 media empire based on print and broadcast shows, and when television and then social media allowed for instant and world-wide communications, the

Huszars watched gape-mouthed as the Kandeskys raked in the money with both hands.

The feud exploded when I showed up. They realized I had the media and business savvy to grow the SNAP empire even larger, and to expand it to Eastern Europe and into Asia, and they lost it. They didn't set out to kill me, they wanted to kidnap me so I could teach them to build a conglomerate to rival SNAP.

Well, that wasn't going to happen. Not if Jean-Louis and all the Kandesky demons could help it. So I got round-the-clock security, which I still thought of as captivity and chafed under. And that reaction drove Jean-Louis into a frenzy, so he stopped confiding in me and just worked with the demons to keep me under their surveillance. Which made me yell at him that he never took my feeling into considerations...which lead to....just say our Dance of the Stupid Egos was alive and smashing up a lot feelings as it lumbered back and forth.

"We haven't cleared up much." I pulled away from him to catch my breath. "Am I, or am I not, going to Moscow?"

"Not. At least not right now. We're going to use some of Markov's contacts in Kiev to begin something in Ukraine first. Test the market. The Russian oligarchy is still being run like a Mafia enterprise, with outward wealth and inward secrecy. We have to figure out how to develop information about all those billionaires.

"And now, I have to get back to Stefan. We have a double agenda with the Huszars tonight. How's the possible coup against Matthais coming along and who's the best contact in Kiev. You're welcome to sit in, but I'll warn you, the conversation will only be in Hungarian and Russian and I won't be able to translate."

It was a sop, but I grabbed it. At least if I were sitting at the table, I had gravitas with the Huszars, and truth-to-tell, with all the Kandeskys as well.

Chapter Eight

I hate meetings. I'm not a person who thinks going to meetings gets things done. I'm much better at one-to-one, make a decision, get it done.

So why I thought sitting in a meeting with a bunch of vampires speaking Russian was going to be interesting, I don't know. I put it down to what Jean-Louis did to me, and tonight he was doing it in spades. He looked glorious.

Dinner tonight wasn't formal, so Jean-Louis had chosen a dark gray pinstripe Armani suit, white shirt, subtly patterned tie, gold cuff links and a gold Patek Phillippe watch so thin that it looked as though it could float away. As we joined the meeting, he took off his jacket and rolled his shirt sleeves back, exposing his beautifully long and expressive hands and wrists. His glimmer was low and his eyes were so black they sparkled with reflected light. It was all I could do to collapse into a chair, not onto the floor.

And that was the high point of the meeting. It went back and forth, with Jean-Louis doing most of the Kandesky talking. Occasionally Alessandr would say something, waving his hand for emphasis, and I took it that he was probably talking about the Neutrality. Jean-Louis would turn to Milos or Bela for clarification.

When Markov spoke, it was Russian and I figured they were discussing the next step in Kiev. Stefan was quietly taking it all in, his eyes missing nothing. Pen sat next to him and the two would exchange a quick whispered consultation about a point then relapse to silent, careful watchfulness.

I managed about an hour-and-a-half. When one of the house demons brought in a tray with water, coffee and Bulls

Blood, the lull gave me a chance to leave with a small lie.

"Please excuse me, I need to check New York emails and voicemails while there's still time today. Baron, Pen, thank you for a lovely dinner, Jean-Louis, would you give my regrets to our guests for leaving?"

Jean-Louis caught my eye with a glance that said "Later". Or I hoped it said "later". It was after two in the morning, and I didn't want him to use up all of his night dealing with the Huszars and other business.

Back in my suite, I changed to my California clothes, jeans and an old shirt of Jean-Louis' that he'd left one morning, grabbed a bottle of water and went into my office. It wasn't a total lie, there were always emails and voicemails from around the world. Keeping up with the Western Hemisphere and the U.S., particularly with the time difference between the coasts, meant I could practically do business any time I chose. Europe was easier, with just three hours to deal with.

Tonight's email stream was a flurry of cc's on feedback from the show, layouts for the next magazine, requests from budding celebs for coverage, letters from PR agents letting us know that their clients would be at this party or that opening and wouldn't we want to send a team to cover it. Jazz and her staff (she now had two assistants and was in middle management heaven; constantly referring to them as "my staff" in a way that always gave me a Biblical connotation), were doing a terrific job at keeping these every-day issues at bay.

Jazz had catalogued the freelancers and paparazzi we used by country and expertise (film and TV stars, aristos, sports figures, politicos, just-plain-filthy-richos) so she had contract templates ready to go. Anyone new, she ran by me to vet. She'd send me work samples, clips or videos, reviews or testimonials, references and any rap sheets. Once they were OK'd we'd buy three or four submission from them. If those turned out well, they got moved to our "approved" status, which meant they could submit stuff, we'd use it (or not) and once a month send them a compilation of everything we bought, with a check.

Also tonight was a nicer, longish, gossipy email from Francois. He was looking forward to me visiting him in Paris and had set up appointments with some of the couturier houses, both for shopping and to talk about coverage for the spring shows. We weren't a fashion mag. Our competition wasn't Vogue or Elle or Glamour. We covered the women who bought and wore those clothes, who attended the shows, and the men who (usually) paid for them.

When we covered the Oscars (or any big celeb event) our writers and photographers had to know who was wearing what, where and when they bought it—or borrowed it, many times—and occasionally did a sidebar on the designer. This was amazing self-fulfillment and everybody won.

I'd only had one chance to visit the Paris houses before I was whisked away to the Hungarian wilds, so I was excited about this trip. I also needed Francois to help me set up the same kind of a junket to Milan for the Italian shows, although the way Jean-Louis bought Armani and Gucci, he'd probably want to go.

I was sidetracking about time in Milan with Jean-Louis and didn't hear the door open, so when Jean-Louis touched my shoulder, I thought my heart would stop—from fear, not lust. Because I jumped so suddenly, he put his hand over my mouth to keep my screams from waking Elise, then leaned over to cover my mouth with his.

That stopped the screams.

This was a ploy he'd developed to keep me from waking up the whole wing of the castle. I have a huge startle reflex, which is deadly when I'm suddenly waked up. There had been a few occasions at the outset of my living here that proved embarrassing all the way around. My screams brought the maid and the demons running, usually with their guns drawn, which brought even more screams from the servants. And about this time, somebody always flipped on all the outside security lights, bathing everything in a weird bluish glow that pretty much woke everybody up except the vampires who were up anyway.

It took an hour of so for everything to settle back down, so the word was out that nobody could just come into my rooms at night without making sure I was awake. Stefan, Jean-Louis and Sandor hoped this was enough of a deterrent that if—or when—I screamed again, it was really a threat . Of course Jean-Louis being Jean-Louis, he handled it in a slightly different way, which was fine by me.

I returned his kiss and wound my arms around his neck.

"I'm surprised you stayed as long as you did at the meeting," He broke away, the corners of his eyes crinkling. "Felt you proved your point?"

I stuck my tongue out at him.

"Ha, that's one of the things I love about you. You're so adult." He stuck his out at me, which cracked us up.

"You're so damned smug, you knew I wouldn't be able to stick with the meeting."

He smiled. "I know, but it meant a lot to you to be there, so there you were. Want to know what happened?"

"Of course I do, but what time is it? How soon before you have to leave?"

"It's only four and sunrise isn't until almost seven."

"Let's talk then. Want something to drink?"

He wiggled his eyebrows. "What are you offering? You?"

"Not hardly. What's happening with the coup?" If I didn't keep the banter light, either we'd end up back in our Stupid Cycle or I'd fall so far under his spell that I'd become a donor, something he'd asked me about but not something I was ever going to think about.

He laid back in the chair and draped one of his long legs over the arm. "Where is the coup going? I'm not sure. Alessandr is energetic, but not one of the brighter Huszars. And that's saying a lot from that bunch, none of whom are very bright. I really need to deal with Karoly, he's got the best handle on manipulation and disinformation. I've loaned him several books and political maneuvers and propaganda."

I was surprised. I'd figured that Karoly and his band of merry vampires were chafing under Matthais' hand and just wanted to exercise a little of their own power. Now Jean-Louis was saying that this may actually look like a regime change. Who was Karoly planning on using disinformation on? His own tribe? The villagers they consistently hunted for food? The lower echelons of the various governments of the area they called their territory?

It must have been hard on the vampire families, keeping track of the political divisions that overlapped their home areas. When they were young, or new, or regulars, the area was all part of the Austro-Hungarian Empire, a huge swath of Central Europe. After World War I, the empire split apart into different countries, a move that was even more complicated after World War II. Bring in the Cold War, the Soviet influence, the breakup of the USSR, and you had some cities that were in seven different countries or political subdivisions, within a hundred years. Trying to remember who to pay off, and in which currency, kept the Huszars on their toes.

But disinformation sounded like they were going to head in a different direction and needed some positive spin on their motives.

"What, exactly, are Karoly and his followers trying to do?"

Jean-Louis waved his hand. "I don't know, but what I'm trying to get them to do, is to become a subsidiary."

"What? You want them to be part of the Kandeskys?" I snorted at the thought. "These are the people—well, not really people, but...you know—who have fought with you for centuries over territory, food, power. And let's not forget that they've had it in for me. Now they'll just come along quietly into the fold? I think not!"

As I stood up, all hell broke loose outside. And this time when I screamed, Jean-Louis didn't stop me.

Unidentified things beat against the side of the building, smashed into the windows and rained soot down the fireplaces.

The outside lights blazed on, showing the terraces and gardens in strobe-like detail. I was torn between rushing to the windows and hiding under the bed covers. As I wavered, Jean-Louis calmly walked to the door and had a quiet conversation with Vladmir. I heard, "Let's give it about five more minutes," before I rushed into the bathroom and locked the door. Even through the door, though, I could hear the shrieks of whatever was attacking, undercut by the deep shouts of the demons. "Over here," "No, toward the river" "I've netted some!"

Suddenly pounding on the bathroom door was louder than the volume of sound and Elise was yelling, "Are you alright?"

"I'm fine," I shouted, then thought better of it and opened the door to her. She was startled, but not frightened, wrapped in a robe, her eyes still heavy with sleep.

"What started the commotion? Were you still up?" She glanced at my jeans-and-shirt outfit. "Didn't Jean-Louis come up tonight?" Nothing if not discreet, our Elise. She was perfectly aware that I was involved with Jean-Louis and that he "visited" me most nights, but it wasn't a subject we discussed.

Jean-Louis. Oh, shit, where was he?

Chapter Nine

I was afraid to look outside. What if Jean-Louis had run out while I'd locked myself in the bathroom like a five-year-old? How was I going to get over this fear? How could I ever stand up to the Kandeskys, let along the Huszars, if I caved at the first sign of trouble?

Standing next to the long windows, now glowing rectangles of blue-white light, I was immobilized with indecision. Me. The one who always acted. One of my mother's mantras rang in my head: *Always make a move. Any move is active, no move is passive and passive, you lose.*

What if I looked out and saw Jean-Louis's body? What if I didn't see his body? What if ...the door almost slammed open and I jumped. No shrieks, but then I probably couldn't be heard. When I managed to open my eyes, Jean-Louis was standing there, grinning at me.

"What are you doing? You son-of-a-bitch! You scared me to death." The string of invective faded off as I watched his grin broaden.

"Ha, I guess it worked."

I was aware the noise was abating and then the lights suddenly snapped off, leaving white scars pulsing on my retinas.

"What worked? What's going on?" I didn't see what he had to grin about.

He came over to me. "I'm sorry, but we couldn't tell you. Your reaction, your honest reaction was a big part of the plan."

Here we went again. Something he couldn't or didn't share with me. Something that scared me out of my wits, and that fright was part of his plan. This was making me crazy and I wasn't sure I wanted any part of it.

I went over and slammed the door shut, almost catching Vladmir's face. By now, I was truly steamed, the fear lending fire to my anger. "That's it, you louse! I'm tired of being thrown to the wolves, or whatever was screeching around out there! I'm leaving in the morning!"

"And where would you go? And how will you get there?" His smugness was unbearable.

"I'll go home, to LA. You forget I have a home there. I'll take a plane!"

"How are you planning to get to the airport? Ask a demon to drive you? Call a cab? And no, I didn't forget you have a home in LA. If you remember, I, we, pay for it."

That brought me up short. He was right. I was all but a prisoner here, and even my home, my safe haven, in reality belonged to the Kandeskys. I backed over to the couch and slumped, worn out with the drain of adrenaline. I looked up at him and began silently to cry.

"On, no, no, no, no..." He was beside me, trying to hold me in his arms. "Oh love, my love, please don't cry, I never meant for you to be hurt."

I tried to turn away from his arms, but he took my shoulders and turned me back to his face. "It was a ploy to get Alessandr and Markov safely back to Huszar territory. We know that the house is constantly under surveillance. You know that, that's why we always have a demon with you. How would it look if two of the younger leaders were seen peacefully leaving the Baron's castle?

"This way, we took Alessandr and Markov out a tunnel that leads into the forest. From there, there's a trail to the Neutrality. When Huszar forces got wind of them, they were entering the Neutrality and could say that they'd been on a reconnaissance mission and just escaped being taken by the Kandesky demons and vampires. Then when the Huszar forces attacked, and you screamed, it all added verity to their story. They went home as heroes and Matthais can't touch them.

"This is what I meant when I said Karoly was beginning

to learn dis- and misinformation. Making something look different from what it is."

He put his hand under my chin and looked at my watery eyes. "I've never seen you cry."

My tears had slowed, but I was left with a very unromantic stuffy nose that was beginning to run. This was a big reason why I didn't cry. It took an armload of anger and frustration to force tears from me.

"Here." Jean-Louis handed me a box of tissues. I wiped my eyes and blew my nose. "I thought that gentlemen always had a handkerchief tucked away to help a crying lady." The words were light but my tone wasn't.

"You've been reading too many romance novels. We may be centuries old but we're aware of basic cleanliness. After all, we have to know about pathogens in bodily fluids."

I managed a weak smile. "You can't just get around me that easily this time. I'm seriously upset that you didn't tell me what was going on. And then," I was building up another head of steam, "when I said I'd leave, you reminded me that you owned me! It's all about business, isn't it!"

This was my big pit of fear, the nagging feeling that Jean-Louis was only interested in me for my commercial value. Not only was I outstanding at my job, I was a magnet for the Huszars, which made me doubly valuable. They could use my expertise to grow their media empire and they could bring their age-old enemies into the fold using me as bait.

"I don't know how to solace you. I'm walking a tightrope between you, the Huszars and the Baron." His beautiful, dark eyes dimmed and his skin began to pale. He suddenly looked old, maybe not his age but enough so that he lost his vitality, and I could make out the bones in his face.

"I am falling in love with you. The Baron—and Pen as well as Carola—are warning me about loving a regular. So the more I try and keep you safe, the more they see me pulling away from the family. Then bring the Huszars into it, and the lines blur between personal and professional. And you get hurt and upset. I'm damned with every step I take."

I took up one of his long, lovely hands. "I can manage a lot if I know that you love me. I think I doubt you because I've never had a love like this, a man like you, a vampire. Until I met you and the Kandeskys, I didn't even believe that vampires existed!"

He turned to me, his glimmer coming back on low. "Please don't doubt what I feel for you. I have no other motive than to love you for as long as we can. Because of my other responsibilities, it may seem as though you're only worth what business you bring in, but that's not the case."

This time when he leaned over to kiss me, it was soft, caring, caressing. I leaned into it and then we both felt the jolt of desire as he slid his tongue into my mouth. His hand stopped caressing my face, dropped down to undo two buttons of the shirt and found my nipple.

With his touch, it began to burn with sharp pleasure. He lifted me and carried me to my bed where we made long, passionate love until the edge of daylight forced him to leave.

Chapter Ten

Francois waved happily as I came down the steps from the Baron's jet. He'd been turned when he was just 21 and retained the ebullience of his age, even though his professionalism made him a star in SNAP management. He headed up both the Paris office and the French language edition of SNAP, so had responsibility for covering a lot in the film, jet-set, Euro-trash wealthy population. Plus, he had the planet's fashion leaders in his orbit, so he was a go-to guy for much of our content.

Tonight, he had a laid on a mini pub-crawl of some spots after a quick tour of the office and introduction to some staffers. He, I, and my bags were in the SNAP Mercedes limo before I realized that Sandor had added others to our party. I could only see the back of his head in the passenger seat, but both this guy and the driver wore signature black suits.

I glanced over to Francois, raised my eyebrows and waved my hand at the two heads. He gave me a Gallic shrug and mouthed two names that I thought were Denis and Michel. Hmmm, two demons in Paris to keep me safe?

The limo pulled through tall double doors and parked in a courtyard of a 19th century building in the 7th Arrondisment. We were herded to an open-cage elevator that only held me, Francois and one of the demons. At the top floor, the elevator grille pulled open and we were in a foyer of a penthouse apartment.

My mouth must have dropped because Francois giggled. "Even now, Maxie, you're surprised at the Baron's arrangements?"

I tore my eyes away from the lighted Eiffel Tower, almost close enough to touch, and nodded. "Is this yours?"

"Non, my apartment is a few blocks away. It's behind the Ecole Miltaire and I'm high enough up that it feels like I'm living in the trees, but nothing as spectacular as this. Visitors are surprised the first time."

"Surprised" didn't cover the reaction. It never occurred to me that a view like this existed. To the right of the Tower, the Seine showed black under its bridges and the lights of the whole of the Right Bank, from the Museum of Man to the Louvre, reflected in the dark water, punctuated by the Ile de la Cite and Norte Dame.

I had to mentally slap myself that I was here on business, although how people did business in this amazing city, I didn't know.

A creak and slamming metal brought me back. The second demon and my bags had arrived. A woman, probably the housekeeper, emerged from another room, spoke rapid French and directed that my bags be taken to a bedroom in the back.

Once done, she came over and Francois introduced her as Marnee, the housekeeper-cum-cook who worked for Paris SNAP. "She's not always here, she also oversees our catering and arrangements for other visitors who stay in various hotels. The Baron brings her here when someone special is visiting."

"Well, am I someone special?"

Francois looked as though he'd stuck his finger in a socket. "Are you special?" His voice came from the bottom of the pond, so he cleared his throat and started again. "Of course, you're special," he managed to get out. "This is where Pen always stays when she's in Paris. And the Baron and Jean-Louis stay here as well."

Hoo, boy, I was in pretty exalted company, then. I nodded as though it was my everyday due and didn't speak. I didn't think I could.

"Do you want to freshen up before we go out? Marnee will show you your rooms."

True to his word, Marnee led me down the hall to a suite with a sitting room, bedroom and bath. The demon had already brought my bags and Marnee had unpacked a few things, so I grabbed my make-up case, went into the bathroom, closed the door and sat on the ledge of the oversize tub, taking slow, deep breaths. I wasn't sure I'd ever get rid of the country-cousin feeling that being around these vampires occasioned.

Once calm and repaired, Francois and I headed out, along with the demons, who were, I found out, indeed Denis and Michel. They nodded when I made Francois introduce me, but didn't shake my hand, None of the more companionable ease that Sandor and I had fallen into, these guys were all business.

We reversed the arrival, Francois and Denis (or maybe Michel) going down in the elevator first then Michel (or Denis) and I followed. One of them started the car remotely, we got in and headed out. Francois let loose with a spate of French and the limo's moon roof slid open as we headed down the Champs Elysees. I'd been to Paris a few times on business trips, but they were always quick and even though SNAP's travel office made the arrangements, I wasn't actually a guest of the Baron. This was different.

We went to three or four clubs, had a late dinner at some small restaurant that knew Francois and always had a supply of steak tartar and Bull's Blood, spent about an hour in the office planning out the next few days and I was escorted back up the elevator by both demons while Francois called for a regular SNAP town car to take him home.

Marnee brought coffee and rolls at noon. Apparently, she was more than a housekeeper, because she also handed me my schedule. At 3, the limo would pick me up and take me to two houses on Blvd. Haussmann. Francois would join me at Haus Etoile, a new and hot designer who was being bought by some of the up-coming stars, we'd have cocktails and come back to the Baron's apartment where I was hosting a dinner party for 30.

Wait a minute, I was hosting?

I needed to call Jean-Louis. Or Francois. Or even Pen. Damn, those vampires, they were all asleep. I looked at Marnee who calmly smiled until she finally understood that I was grimacing from terror. She started on an explanation. When I stammered out "Plus lentment, s'il vous-plaît," she realized that my French was thoroughly inadequate and said, in English, "It's all arranged. The guests will be here by 10 this evening. You and Francois will be back by 9, giving you plenty of time to change. Francois has the guest list and will go over it with you on the way back."

My mouth was opening and closing without a sound. These vampires were past masters at having guests, dinner-parties for 30 or 40, cocktail parties for 100, weekend house parties. I'm from California. Some of my parties consisted of barbequing hamburgers on the deck of my condo.

Marnee patted my hand. "Everything will be fine. Do you want to bathe or shower?" She went into the closet to pick out some clothes.

I opted for the shower, hoping the driving water would pound some courage into me. This would be OK. My God, I was upper management in the world's largest media company. How many parties, openings, galas, had I been to, or covered? How many times had the Baron and Pen hosted guests at the castle while I'd been living there?

There was a difference. At many of those events, I'd either been working, which allowed me to wrap up in my SNAP Boss persona, or I was with Jean-Louis, who moved through these gatherings like a fish through water. This was my first time solo. I had to suck it up.

Just like the Swiss railways, the schedule ticked off until Francois and I were in the limo headed for the Baron's and I felt as though I could unburden myself. Luckily, two glasses of wine during cocktails had numbed my panic.

"How did this dinner party get put together? I didn't even arrive until last night!"

"It was planned a few days ago, right after your travels plans were firm. Jean-Louis and the Baron thought you needed to be seen on your own. It will give you gravitas when you begin to work with the boys from the East."

Ah, the boys from the East. Everything I'd heard about these oligarchs had been that they refused to do business with women. There were a few exceptions, and with women heading up the U.S. State Department recently, they were grudgingly accepting a newer way, but a woman still had barriers to overcome before she was trusted. Well, this was another persona I'd have to adopt if I wanted to keep my place with SNAP.

"That's very sophisticated thinking, thank you. But why wasn't I told earlier?"

Francois gave one of his shrugs that could mean, "who knows", "who cares", "I don't know" or "why are you asking?" In this case, I found out it was "why are you asking the obvious?" when he said "I suspect they want you to get used to handling surprises. When you start getting involved with Kiev and Moscow, most things are surprises and they want to make sure you can manage when the sand shifts."

Once again, I read the situation through my own fears and perspective. They wanted me to take charge. Well, now, this was something I could do.

Chapter Eleven

The dinner party came off without a hitch. The apartment was filled with flowers, the food was delicious, Marnee had gotten a staff together and the guests, primarily French media types, with two young actors, were charmed and charming. I even had time for a quick call to Jean-Louis, but this time I behaved like a grown-up.

"Thank you for the vote of confidence and for having my back."

A low chuckle came through the phone. "You are so American! 'Having your back?' What weird American coined that phrase?"

I wasn't going to let him get to me. Not tonight. "It's a term about danger, it means..."

"Actually, I do know what it means. It's just that you, your countrymen, bring slang and street talk into the everyday language. It's just different. Are you liking Paris?"

"You know I love this city. I really haven't done much today, some looking at a couple of houses, but tomorrow I'm going to spend time with the Parisians."

"Just be careful and remember that Denis and Michel need to be with you at all times."

"I know. I'm talking about being out during the day. I'll be careful."

"Good." Jean-Louis' voice got lower and caressed me, making my face tingle. "I want you to know that I love you, and that some day, soon, you and I will be in Paris together."

His voice and his love wrapped around me and gave me the extra boost that let me sail through the dinner party.

I didn't let the euphoria completely dull my business

sense, though. The two French actors, both beautiful young women, went into my mental "New Talent" folder and after the guests left, I talked to Francois about them.

"I thought you'd pick up on them. I made sure they got invitations. They were stunned at getting invitations to a SNAP do, and awed by you."

I said good-bye to Francois at 3 a.m., the middle of the afternoon for him. I didn't ask what he was going on to do. I wasn't sure if he was gay or bi or hetero. We always laughed and flirted and he usually picked up on some of the most beautiful regular women at parties, but I wanted to make sure that his personal life was his own.

The next day, I announced to Marnee, and Denis and Michel that I was going out to meet some Parisians. By myself.

Denis and Michel wrinkled their eyebrows and had a rapid conversation, this time in Hungarian. Oh-oh, that could mean trouble.

One of them, I was pretty sure it was Denis, went into the office and I could hear lots of beeps that meant an international call. There was a rushed conversation, again in Hungarian, and he came back and said, "No."

I stared at him. It wasn't in their purview to give me orders.

"You don't have the right to tell me no."

"Maybe not me, but Jean-Louis does."

"How did he tell you? It's day time. He's..."

"He should be sleeping, but there are standing orders to wake him if it concerns you. Sandor did. He said that Jean-Louis said 'no'. You must take at least one of us with you. I'll go. Where are you going?"

This was a long conversation with a demon. As usual, I was overridden. We headed for the river by way of the Place de la Resistance. There were still buildings with pockmarks from World War II street fights and each had a plaque with the Resistance Fighter's name.

I loved this. For the first time in months, I'd left the

rarified atmosphere of the Baron and the SNAP executives and just had a chance to be an anonymous onlooker. It was an overcast fall day and the Parisians were wrapped in scarves with umbrellas handy, but the cool mist wasn't keeping anyone inside. The streets were full of people who glanced at Denis with interest, nodded and went on. Not a lot of people strolled along the Seine with a large, powerful guy in a black suit, but they registered him as a bodyguard and left it at that.

We crossed on the Alexander III bridge and continued to the Tuileries, where kids pushed small boats in the ponds, watched by their nannies.

I suddenly wanted to go to Notre Dame. I'm not religious, but that huge Gothic building, girded by flying buttresses and frosted with gargoyles, was too much to miss.

"Let's take the Metro," and I headed down at the Louvre station before Denis could tell me no. He followed me gamely, not wanting to create a scene. We changed at Chatelet for the line to the Ile de la Cite and Denis was less that a step away from me the entire time. I knew I was making him careful? nervous? wary? , but I was having a great time people watching and listening to French pouring over me like a waterfall.

When the train came, Denis and I were jostled apart by a group of Gypsy women with children in tow. The women started an argument at the top of their voices, not watching the kids who ran up and down the car.

Denis edged close to me. "This is a group of pickpockets and bag thieves. Please watch yourself," he said in my ear.

When we left the apartment, I'd stuffed a bunch of euros in the front pocket of my jeans, so felt impervious to trained sticky little hands, but I nodded to Denis.

We came up at the Cite station on the edge of the flower market. I headed off to look at the stalls, now filled with fall wreaths and dried stalks, assuming that Denis would follow. When I turned to head to another stall, a large man caught me eye.

He was a series of muscle slabs, beginning at his head which merged into his shoulders without an indication of a neck. His arms stood out from his body, his hands were huge, with hairy knuckles. He had hair pushing out of the neck and sleeves of his shirt and the only hairless place was his head, smooth-shaven.

His mouth twisted into a grimace, then I realized he was smiling at me. I gave a quick smile back and turned the corner of the stall, only to realize that I'd come into a narrow walkway between the backs of the stalls and the wall of an old stone building. Just as I started back, he turned the corner too, smiled and snatched my arm.

"Ah, lady, you make mistake, yes?"

His English was heavily accented and guttural, probably from an Eastern European country. He wore a Parisian workman's smock over his shirt and pants and smelled like garlic and cheap wine. And I was pretty sure he wasn't going to just give me directions back to the Metro.

As he pulled me into his chest, I managed to shout for Denis before he threw a stinking burlap bag over my head. Then I was lifted, the wind was knocked out of me and I was being carried; not too far before I was dumped onto the ancient cobblestones so hard that my head hit the pavement.

I don't know if I saw stars. I knew I was experiencing what law enforcement calls "altered consciousness", usually the result of too much illegal substances. Mine was altered because I was so groggy I had no idea where I was or who I was with.

Somebody pulled the bag off me, I sucked in a breath of clean air and started coughing. I squeezed my eyes shut and concentrated on just breathing. I could hear voices over me and they finally sorted themselves out to Denis and Michel talking to a guy with a heavy accent, but I must have still been semi-conscious because the words didn't make any sense.

Until I realized they were speaking a language I'd never heard before.

I opened my eyes. I was sitting on the burlap bag,

against the stone wall of a building, looking at the back of a flower stall. Hmmm, I may have been gone for a while, but I hadn't gotten far. Above me, Denis and Michel were talking low and hard to the guy in the smock, who wasn't saying too much back.

Two more demons popped up. They managed to get a needle into the smock guy and when he slumped, unconscious, they poured some more wine over him and strong-armed him away to a waiting car. Denis tsked-tsked and in French, very loudly, said something about people who were drunk during the day.

He then stood me up. "Are you going to be all right?"

"I'm fine, now. I am so sorry, I've gotten you in trouble with Jean-Louis, haven't I? I don't know what happened. The last time I looked, you were right behind me."

"I was, but a swarm of those kids came through, you turned a corner and, poof. It was just enough time for the Chechen to grab you."

"Chechen? Why him, them, those people?"

"We're going to ask him. We think maybe the Russians hired him." Denis' voice was grim. "I'm taking you home. We have another car here."

"Wait, who are those other demons. They are demons, aren't they? Where'd they come from?"

"When I saw you'd been grabbed, I called Michel and had him get back-up. Michel got here first in one car, they came in a second one."

"How did they get through traffic so fast?" I'd seen the parking lot that passes for Parisian traffic first hand.

"You were unconscious for a few minutes. And we all know shortcuts and ways to get around."

He at least allowed me the dignity of walking to the car idling at the curb. For the crowds of people, Parisians and tourists, who were wandering around the Ile de la Cite that day, the demons handled the whole incident so well that no one was aware of what had happened.

"I guess my visit to Notre Dame is off. I can't get Jean-Louis to take me, the vampires get edgy around the church."

"Huh," Denis responded, not amused at my levity.

Chapter Twelve

I was right, Jean-Louis wasn't happy.

Denis (the rat) had already called him and before we got back to the apartment I had a message. My bags were packed, the car was ready, the plane would be at Orly shortly and my Parisian adventure was over.

It was no use arguing with anyone, all of the staff here, demons as well, were just staff and followed Jean-Louis' orders. By nightfall, I was on the way to Orly, but I gave one last shot at Francois.

"I'm sorry Maxie," his voice had lost most of its cheerfulness. "Jean-Louis is very angry and I have to agree with him. We had no idea how closely you were being watched. And we also didn't know about the Chechens. I'll see you at the castle in a few days. We're being called to a family meeting."

My God, this was truly serious. Stefan and Jean-Louis didn't call an all-family meeting often, this was only the second one I knew about.

Chagrinned, I got on the plane and tried to have THE conversation with Jean-Louis. I failed. I knew he was royally angry, and he had every right to be. I'd talked Denis into doing something against his better judgment and now he was in the soup, because of me and with me.

Denis wouldn't be fired, you couldn't fire a demon, but he'd be sent to some way-off-the-beaten-track post with all the time in the world to contemplate his mistake. Sort of a demon limbo where he'd stay until he could do enough good to get back his standing with the family.

Me? Well, me, I *could* get fired.

Good-bye to SNAP and my career I'd worked so hard for. And, oh my god, good-bye to Jean-Louis. I knew I couldn't live without him, I would shrivel and die.

By the time I got into the car for the drive to the castle, my insides were a void. I was beyond sad, beyond frightened. I'd reached numb and resigned. I was going to purgatory, a life of abject misery. I'd gambled *everything* for a few hours of freedom and the worst part was that I hadn't even realized I was gambling.

There was no use talking to the demon Sandor had sent as my escort. He was one I'd never met before, so I guessed I was so far down on the list I'd been assigned the dregs.

When we drove up to the castle, lights were on but there was no welcoming committee. Instead, I was ushered up to my suite, where Elise silently took my bags from the demon.

"Are you hungry? I have some soup."

Soup! It might as well be bread and water. Wasn't I even going to get a last meal? "No, thank you, Elise. I don't think I can eat. I would like a bath, though."

My departure from Paris had been so sudden that I hadn't even felt the remains of my manhandling by the Chechen, but now, after planes and cars and stress and sitting, my muscles were tying themselves in knots and the lump on the back of my head was incredibly sore.

I soaked for maybe half an hour, until I heard Jean-Louis' voice in my sitting room. I certainly wasn't going to talk to him from the bathroom, and not naked, so I climbed out, toweled off and threw on some clothes before I opened the door.

He turned and looked at me. I couldn't tell what his expression meant. His great, dark eyes were hooded, his glimmer was gone, his skin pale and drawn with two small hectic spots of color high on his cheeks. His face was furrowed with lines and wrinkles I'd never seen before. He said, "Maxie".

If he'd stabbed me, it wouldn't have hurt any more that just that one word. I fainted.

When I came to, I had pressure on my arm. Was I tied up? It resolved itself into a blood pressure cuff and I was in my bed with a doctor sitting beside me.

"I don't think she has serious damage," he said to someone else in the room. "I think what we're seeing is the remains of a concussion from when her head hit the cobblestones. We need to watch her, but I don't think it's serious enough to get her an MRI. Beyond the concussion, she has some bruising on her rib cage and a few scrapes. I'd guess it's from being slung around. A couple of Vicodin and she should be fine tomorrow."

"Thank you." Jean-Louis' voice. Noncommittal. The doctor took off the cuff, packed everything away, put two pills on the bedside table and left.

Left me with Jean-Louis.

I looked up at him. "I've never fainted before." What a great opening line!

He shook his head, his beautiful hair falling across his dark eyes. "I don't even know where to start."

"Well, do I still have a job?"

At that, he actually smiled and a slight glimmer highlighted his face.

"You are beyond belief. You're attacked, injured, found by enemies we didn't even know we had, put a hitch in our negotiations with the Huszars and the only thing you can ask about is your job?"

"I figure you're so mad that you'll dump me, but at least I can manage if I still have a job."

"Dump you? Oh lord, woman, speak English! If you mean I'm not interested in you any more, that's not true."

Well, here was a thin shaft of hope. But what kind of interest did he have? I could still be the chum the Kandeskys were using to attract the disaffected Huszars. I could still be used to start the Eastern European version of SNAP. I could still be used as a cautionary tale of how not to behave.

His next words stunned me.

"You persist in thinking that I have some kind of schoolboy crush on you. That my feelings for you are temporary. I've told you that I love you. It's not something I planned, and I don't know how I can make it work, but it's not temporary or easy or light."

He turned toward the windows, pale with moonlight. "I'm most concerned about what may happen in a few years, as you age and I don't. You may decide that you're not comfortable looking older than me. And eventually, you'll die...I won't. I need to be prepared for that. But dump you? No, not in the cards."

Hmmmm. I guess I hadn't lost Jean-Louis so that meant I'd lost my job. Giving up my heart or my soul; not a choice I was happy about.

"Who will you get to replace me? Jazz is doing a wonderful job, but I don't think she knows enough to tackle the expansion."

He whirled around and his expression frightened me. "What are you talking about?" His jaw was set and the words hissed out like venom.

"Well, I know you've called a family meeting, Francois said he'd see me then. I figure the agenda is to find my replacement. I've endangered the family again and brought new threats."

"Yes, all that is true. But not unexpected, you ninny. We just didn't expect it to happen in Paris, or this early, but now that it has, we may have to shift our plans slightly. We thought the Huszars would find some lowlifes to work for them, and they have. Because we're looking at Ukraine and Russia, who better than traditional rabble rousers like the Chechens."

I wasn't completely following his comments. I was so astonished that I couldn't get past the facts that I wasn't fired, that I hadn't lost my lover. If I wasn't going to be punished in some way, then what the hell *was* happening?

My stupefied expression stopped him. "Why are you looking so dumbfounded? What did you expect?"

Here was a question I could answer. "I expected...I expected...that you'd be so angry, that...er...hummmm...I don't know what I expected. That you were so disgusted with me you didn't want me around either personally or professionally."

"You're stammering. That's interesting." His tone was clinical. "I've never seen you at a loss for words. I guess this little fiasco made an impression."

Okay, the gloves were off. "Little fiasco? I try to have a normal few hours, even taking a demon with me, get abducted, pummeled on, slung around like a feed sack, end up with a concussion, hustled out of Paris like a crook, greeted like a paroled prisoner..."

He was actually grinning. "I was pretty sure that would get a rise out of you! I don't like seeing you acting like a whipped dog. Now, do you want to discuss this like two intelligent adults?"

A few minutes ago, I was devastated, thinking that Jean-Louis might want me out of his life. Now I was so pissed that I felt like walking. "You are impossible. I never met anyone so hard to understand and figure out. Why did I get such a chilly reception when I got here? And Elise? Offering me soup? It might as well have been bread and water, the message was so clear. And you! Where were you?"

"Oooh, I love it when your blood is up." He snickered at his bad pun. "Not that I owe you any explanations, but we were in the village, meeting with some of the rest of the family. If we can't get Karoly and his followers set up to take on Matthais, the villagers, and that part of the family, will be the first causalities. They need to understand what we're doing and agree to the next steps. We couldn't just cancel to handle your little to-do and sudden arrival from Paris.

"And don't for a minute think that Huszar hangers-on weren't watching. If we'd rushed back to take care of you, Matthais would think that the Chechen attack had a big impression on us and he'd up the tension."

"You people," I was almost hissing myself, now. "You

people are just like onions! You peel off layers and underneath, there are more layers! It's like trying to find my way through a house of mirrors! Nothing is what it seems."

"Ah, and how do you think we've survived and prospered for centuries? Everyone talks about Byzantine politics. Who do you think we learned from?"

There it was again. I was up against four or five centuries of experience in developing trade and business agreements, in making pacts with various enemies and forging and undoing alliances. And not just the vampires. They'd been around to watch and learn for 500 years of European countries slaughtering each other. No wonder they didn't take people into their confidence easily.

Chapter Thirteen

Now that I knew I wasn't going to lose either my job or Jean-Louis, I relaxed enough that the pain pills kicked in.

"Stay with me love, I think I'm going to collapse" I managed to get out before my head hit the pillow. The next I knew, Elise was hovering in the doorway.

"What's the matter?"

"Hello, Maxie, I didn't want to disturb you. Jazz has been calling."

"How long have I been out?"

"Almost twelve hours, it's afternoon."

My ribs and head tried to resist when I sat up and slid out of bed, but the only way to get through the pain was to get active, so I asked Elise for coffee and headed to the bathroom. A hot shower helped some, Elise's coffee helped more and in a few minutes I was talking to Jazz. It was awkward with the time difference, but she'd stayed up waiting for my call.

"Oh-my-god, Maxie, I'm so glad to hear your voice." Jazz' SoCal breathless speech pattern felt homey and comfortable. "I kept getting these weird, cryptic e-mails and messages that something happened to you in Paris. Some people thought you were dead, or you'd been kidnapped. I even had another show call and ask me if I been tapped to replace you! It's been a zoo around here!"

"Hah, the rumors of my death! I'm here and OK."

"Tell, tell, what happened?"

"You know the Kandeskys and Jean-Louis, they must have been the models for the Official Secrets Act or the CIA. Getting a straight answer out of them is, well, it's just not gonna happen. The gist of it is that I went off, with Denis in tow, to spend a couple of hours just looking. I wanted to go to Notre Dame, and that's not high on the vampire tour list. I guess the Huszars hooked up with some of the Chechen thugs and I was, am, being watched. It only took a few seconds for me to get separated from Denis and, wham, I'd been grabbed."

"Did they get you away?"

"No, Denis, and then Michele, were right there. The Chechen dropped me, I whacked my head on the cobblestones, have a slight concussion and am embarrassed as hell. Every time I want to do something normal, some stupid gangster type moves in on me. I'm getting pretty tired of it and I know Jean-Louis is too."

"Now that I know you're OK, we need to do something about these rumors."

"Yep. Can you draft a release that says I slipped on the street while visiting Notre Dame, have been looked at by a doctor and am resting comfortably for a day before going back to work?"

"You bet. What's next?"

"Add that I'm gong to Kiev next week to begin talks for the Eastern European edition of SNAP and will be looking for talent and staff."

Silence. Then Jazz' voice whispered, "Maxie, do you think that's smart? You were just attacked and now you want to announce where you'll be next week? They'll be waiting for you!"

"Jazz, they'll be waiting for me anyway. Jean-Louis won't cop to it, but I know that he knows the Huszars have me watched probably as close as the demons watch me. I wouldn't be surprised if they have my bathroom here tapped."

Jazz sounded like a vacuum, sucking air. "They wouldn't!"

"Well, they would if they could, but I'm pretty sure they can't. But if I can't get answers from Jean-Louis about what's going on, I'm just going to have to head out on my own."

We hung up, I tackled more than 200 e-mails and felt

well enough to put on some jeans, pick up a couple of demons and head outside for some air. Sandor wouldn't let me out with only one guard, so I had Vladmir and a new one, Vassily. It felt like a parade with the short bit of fresh air uneventful and calming.

I was dressing for dinner when Vladmir pounded on my door then let Jean-Louis in. "Why are we on some kind of amusement park roller coaster?"

His voice was light, but his eyes were sparking.

"I don't know what you mean."

"You're about as innocent as a blizzard. You're whipping around, piling up snow so deep that you think I can't find you. What kind of game are you playing, Miss 'I'm gong to Kiev next week'?"

"What? Can't I do my job?"

"Why did you announce it to the world before checking with me, er, us?"

"I didn't think I needed your permission to set up business meetings."

That stumped him.

"Of course not." He was flustered and backpedaled. "It's just that, well, I need to, that is Sandor and I need to schedule the guards and make arrangements."

Oh right, Jean-Louis was going to make my travel reservations? That pig wasn't flying. What else was going on?

"I announced it 'to the world' because I wanted the world to know that I was fine and that a little fall in Paris wasn't going to stop me from doing the job I was hired to do; set up an edition of SNAP to serve Eastern Europe. I'm scouting locations. Since I'm apparently being watched all the time by hired thugs—at least I figure that the Chechen was on the Huszar payroll—it won't matter if I announce it, they'll know anyway!

"Are we going down to dinner?"

Jean-Louis looked at me. I couldn't tell what his expression meant, but he finally pursed his lips and blew out a sigh.

"Let's go. I hate to admit it but you're right, if this were just your normal job, I wouldn't have a say in where or when you went. I have trouble keeping my personal emotions out of it."

"Tell you what, I'll check with you if you'll let me in on all your doings with the Huszars. And that doesn't mean sitting for hours in meetings, listening to you guys speak Hungarian or any other Slavic languages."

I grabbed a Pashmina shawl, almost knocking over a table lamp as I slung it around my shoulders, and stomped out the door. This time, Vladmir knew enough and stood back as I came through. He nodded at Jean-Louis. Did the demons talk about me when I wasn't around? Swap stories of how difficult I was? Wonder how Jean-Louis put up with me?

Not my problem.

Chapter Fourteen

My pre-dinner barb must have made an impression. After dinner, a small family affair with just the Baron, Pen, Carola, Bela, Jean-Louis and me, we moved into a small salon for a true meeting.

Pen and Carola started it off, surprisingly taking my side.

"You think you're taking care of Maxie when you keep her in the dark about your plans. But that's just trivializing her feelings, treating her like child." Pen was serenity itself as these strong words dropped into the room.

Carola took it up. "I imagine that you're still reacting to Magda's murder. You probably think that you didn't do enough to keep her safe. The truth is, you can't lead people's lives for them. If you keep a plant safe in a closet, it won't get stolen, but it will die. Maxie is a grown, intelligent woman, traits that make her so valuable to us.

"You have to remember that those traits make her valuable to the Huszars, as well. What we, you, need to do is work with Maxie, bring her in on all our planning and the meetings with the Huszars. If she's a participant in the plans, she'll be safer and we'll have the benefit of her point of view."

Jean-Louis had the grace to look abashed. "I have been reliving Magda's slaughter and it's making me vulnerable."

He turned to me and for the first time in days, his glimmer washed across his face, filling all the dark places and hollows with a fine light like stardust. "Welcome to the family council, Maxie."

All the teenage angst, the drama queen antics, the snittiness, drained from me. "Thank you, Jean-Louis. And thank all of you. Pen and Carola, you understood exactly what I've been trying to say. I want to work with you and make SNAP and this new venture take off."

I looked around. Now that the nicey-niceys were over, the vampires were intense, turning their energies onto the puzzle of the Huszars.

Jean-Louis took the lead. "I've been getting together with Karoly every day to help him with disinformation. We have to rely on word-of-mouth, but the rumor-mill is starting to move even faster. We need to encourage Karoly to actively recruit more Huszars, and to make sure he brings in members from all branches of the family."

"All branches? I thought the Huszars were only here, in Hungary?" My confusion must have shown on my face.

"Well, their main family is here," Carola began in her light voice. "They aren't nearly as diversified and spread as we are, but they do have smaller branches in Europe. And one of the reasons we're pushing Jean-Louis to make you a partner in knowledge is that a major branch is in Russia and Ukraine."

The Baron took up the story. "When the Cossacks, as well as other Russian Imperial troops, were running pograms throughout the edges of Eastern Europe, the Huszars were right along with them. That family..." he broke off in disgust and shook his head then continued, "Wherever there's been death and disturbances, the Huszars have been there. I don't think they're smart enough to have stirred up troubles themselves, but they are the ultimate hangers-on. They'd send scouts out to all the major cities in Central and Eastern Europe to watch the pulse of the people. The minute they spotted trouble, they moved a small group in, to feed off the losers.

"Those small groups took some pressure for food off of the main branch of the family, the ones still here in Hungary, and allowed the native population of the area to successfully breed. It was a strategy to keep food resources available."

I was stunned. Not because the Huszars had spread out, but because the Baron spoke so casually about the peasant population as a food resource. Of course I knew that the

Huszars, and vampires everywhere, lived off blood, and usually ended up killing their victims. I just hadn't followed that through to its logical conclusion.

I looked at them. "Is this how you view all humans? As a renewable food source?"

There was a chorus of gasps and denials then Pen spoke. "I'll put that rudeness down to the fact that you're still naive about the world and proper behavior. Of course we don't view humans as renewable food. If we did, do you think that we'd be in the business we're in?"

A good point.

"The Huszars are boors, uneducated and uncultured. That does not make their behavior the standard for all vampires." Jean-Louis' voice was tight, a sign he'd taken umbrage. "We saw from the beginning that killing our neighbors was not the best plan for the long run and began recruiting donors and developing substitutes. By using raw animal meat and blood, we were able to cut down our consumption of human blood. Usually, some every month or so will keep us healthy, and the donors can easily supply that. Of course it's much easier in these days of refrigeration and fast, reliable transportation."

Now the Baron broke in again. "We're discussing this now because beginning tomorrow, when you go to Kiev, you'll be going into the areas that were part of the Huszar expansion a few hundred years ago."

"And you need to know that you'll be watched by some of the Huszar family as well as their paid goons, the Chechens and whoever else they've been able to scratch up. I want you safe and I want you to heed our warnings." Jean-Louis' glimmer was coming back.

I nodded to all of them. "Thank you for including me in your confidences. I will watch my behavior and not act so rashly. I don't want to endanger any of the demons or any of you.

"Now, please excuse me, I'm going to my apartment to pack."

Jean-Louis didn't follow me upstairs.

Chapter Fifteen

Kiev.

The ancient city on the Dnieper River.

Land of,...what? I didn't know.

Like much of the old Soviet Union, Kiev and Ukraine were still little known in the West. My most vivid recollection was that Kiev was the closest large city to the nuclear disaster at Chernobyl. And that made me anxious.

On the plane, I'd done some research. It turned out that Kiev was really an ancient city, with its beginnings as a trade center in the 5th century. It had seen the Vikings come and make it their capital of the Rus, and suffered complete destruction under the Mongols in the 13th century. It resurfaced during the 19th century industrial revolution and had been the capital of Ukraine for the past 75 years or so.

It had a population of about 3 million and was the third largest city in the old USSR, so it was a logical choice for a SNAP bureau. I asked Cheri, the cabin attendant and one of the SNAP girls—pale skin, Russian Red lipstick, no doubt a donor—to have the pilot circle before we landed. From the air, Kiev was reminiscent of Budapest; straddling a river with industry and commerce on one bank and residential areas on the other.

I was met by Taras Chemenkov, a businessman and journalist we'd tapped as the first bureau chief. He was experienced and had been the freelance Ukrainian correspondent for several of the weekly news magazines, including the World Report. Of course, the real power was the Kandesky family member Nikoly, a vampire I'd never met. He was in the backseat of the Mercedes limo. Taras and I piled in,

Vladmir and Vassily got in front with the driver—another demon?—and we headed into town.

"Is this your first visit to Kiev?" Taras spoke good English, with a trace of Slavic intonation. If he'd been writing for Western magazines, he must have been able to speak several languages.

"Yes, and I'm surprised that it reminds me so much of Budapest. Your English is very good, what other languages do you speak?"

"Russian, of course, German, French, Ukrainian."

"Not Hungarian?"

"No." Nikoly broke in, his voice silky and low. "I speak Hungarian, so I translate anything from the Baron for Taras. We need Taras' skills in languages we use for business, not communication with the family."

Lord, had I put my foot in it already? As a regular, Taras wasn't far enough up the chain of command for family discussions. I was never sure in this game of friend or foe and shifting alliances. It was like trying to capture smoke. Just when I had it all thought out, understood and safely packaged, somebody new popped up. When I got back to the castle, I was going to pin Jean-Louis down and get a complete cheat sheet from him of who was who. And an organizational chart as well, even though it was tricky because some of the family members who worked for SNAP actually reported to regulars, like me, so there weren't lines of supervision...more like circles on a Venn diagram.

"Hummmm. What else is in your job description?"

I couldn't see Nikoly's eyes behind his enormous dark glasses, but the corner of his mouth lifted slightly. "I handle the logistical interface for the supply chain."

What?

"What? I'm not sure what that means." I was trying to keep a stupid expression off my face. This guy may be a vampire and a member of the Kandesky family, but he spoke like a newly-minted MBA.

This time Taras translated for me. "I'm the bureau chief. I make all the assignments, decide on the coverage. I'll be working with you on the mock-up of the Slavic edition and making sure all the print tallies with the broadcast. Nikoly is the one who will work with all the technical people, the government folks, and..."

"And the Russian Mafia, the Chechens and others. This is Eastern Europe, it doesn't work like the West. After the Soviets, there's been a vacuum of power. I'm the one who works in the vacuum." This time there was a definite smile.

Ah, the clean-up man. Now him being a Kandesky family member made sense. He had the juice, backed by the Baron's money and all the demons, to get things done.

"Will it require a lot to get the bureau up and running?"

"We've been working on it for a few months now." Taras nodded. "We'll drop your bags at the hotel then give you a tour."

We pulled up to the forecourt of the Premier Palace Hotel and I gasped. What I'd expected was probably some radiation-dusted Econolodge. What I got was a grand European hotel. Shades of the Sacher in Vienna, George V in Paris or the Grand Bretagna in Athens. It took up an entire block and looked like a Victorian wedding cake.

"This is wonderful. I usually stay at apartments owned by SNAP or the Baron, but this is lovely. I'm changing my mental image of Kiev."

Taras giggled. "A lot of our visitors are surprised that we have amenities. This is part of the kind of information we want to get out. Attracting celebrities will make our job easier."

"And it may dilute the power of the oligarchs and their boys." Nikoly's voice was light, but the words held menace.

Once in my suite, I freshened up and then the demon parade followed me back to the limo where Nikoly was waiting.

"Where's Taras?" I looked around.

"He's gone to the offices to make sure everything is ready for your visit. I wanted to have a few moments with you alone." I got in, the demons took their places in the front, the communication window zipped up and Nikoly said, "Jean-Louis told me about the Chechen attack in Paris"

Damn the man! I thought we were all going to hand out the story of a slip-and-fall. Like any good vampire, Nikoly read my body language, or maybe the waves of anger I was sending off, because he held up a hand.

"No one knows about the true event beside me. Jean-Louis and the Baron felt I needed to know because I'm here, in the home of the thugs. We're hoping that I can trace the money and the orders and find out who's hired the Chechens."

"The Huszars have hired them!"

"Well, yes. But who exactly? And what are they planning to do? And many times when one hires them, the employees take over the business. They have a history of going off on their own when they smell money. There's not a lot of money with the Huszars, but with the Kandeskys..."

He didn't need to say any more. I was reading this picture, and it wasn't a pretty one. The Chechens were after me. The Huszars had put out a contract. But now, the Chechens may have made a target of their own.

Where was my quiet bedroom overlooking the ocean in Santa Monica? Where were my friends, the warm afternoons of coffee in Westwood, even zany Venice Beach?

Nikoly looked over at me. "Do you want to quit? Jean-Louis told me you weren't the quitting type."

Chapter Sixteen

Of course I wasn't the quitting type. But I was, for damn sure, the scared type.

I took a deep breath. "Okay, let's go to the SNAP offices."

"We're here." Nikoly gestured to a very modern steel and glass building several stories high that wouldn't have looked out of place in Century City. Workers on scaffolds were busy attaching the SNAP mirrored logo to the outside and when I walked in, I was met with an ice-blond SNAP girl as the receptionist behind the black marble counter.

Her Russian Red mouth smiled but her blue eyes stayed cold. "And you are?"

"I am Maximilla Gwenoch, the Managing Editor of SNAP," I snapped. Really, didn't anyone call ahead?

At least she had the grace to smile at me with her eyes this time. "I'm sorry Ms. Gwenoch, we expected you to come in the employees entrance. Let me page Taras for you." She murmured into her earbud while the phone gurgled then said "Taras' assistant will be right out."

Sure enough, a dark-haired young woman wearing four-inch stilettos came through the wall of mirrors behind the reception desk and said, "Follow me." I assumed she said that, because she waved me in, but she wasn't speaking English. Like Alice, like L.A., I walked into the mirror.

The interior offices were much quieter and smaller than home, but the designer had spent time making the look-and-feel as close to L.A. as he could. There were probably 10 people working in cubicles, phones gurgled, voices spoke a variety of languages.

Taras was standing in front of his office, tucked away in a back corner. "Welcome to the Kiev bureau. Do you like it?"

"'"I do. It reminds me of home."

"We had our designer come in and shoot a lot of video of the headquarters, and used that as our plan. We even have an attached garage and employee entrance." He nodded as Nikoly came through an access door.

"What are you planning as a premiere?"

"I'm glad you asked that. Working with the oligarchs is difficult. They have money rolling out of their pores, but they're very private. They spend their money on huge houses, cars, second homes on the Continent or in America and on bodyguards. They hire armies of bodyguards. If you have money in this post-Soviet era, you're a target for bunches of thugs looking to kidnap you. And they're not picky, kind of like the Somali pirates. Anybody who can pay the ransom is fair game."

"Well, that's going to make finding and reporting on celebrities a little hard. Do you have plans?"

"That's where part of my job in the vacuum comes in." Nikoly waved us into an empty office and took a seat on a couch. "Much of the social scene is in private, at homes and clubs, and I'm in charge of finding where they are and getting us in the door."

"Do you have a lot of freelance talent?"

Taras nodded. "I still have some good contacts from my freelancing days. Here it's not enough just to hang out in front of somebody's house. All you get are pictures of blackened limo windows or, if you're lucky, the bodyguard's profile. There are some clothing designers who are coming up, there's a small film culture, and then we do a lot of trades. People are interested in celebrities from other places, primarily movie stars, so we use copy from the U.S. and send them, you, what we can get."

What he said about the nouveau-rich was true. Even in the media-hungry, paparazzi crazy U.S. most of the Eastern Europeans buying property stayed under the radar. One sale of a New York apartment, for a reputed $38 million, was only reported as being purchased for the 22-year-old daughter of a Russian billionaire. She was attending college in the city.

The highest price ever paid for a single family home in the U.S., $100 million for a 25,500 square foot mansion in Los Altos Hills, on the San Francisco Peninsula, was to Yuri Milner, a Russian with investments in Twitter and Facebook. But you never saw these people in any of the magazines or on any of the network or cable shows that followed celebrities.

Well, there were a lot of people interested in what the movers and shakers of Ukraine, Russia and the Baltic states were doing. People around the world didn't just live their own lives any more, witness the role the social media had in the north-African Arab uprisings.

And we at SNAP didn't care about the politics, just about the people. What they were doing, who they were seeing, what they were wearing, where they were going.

"We'll figure it out." Taras and Nikoly shared a glance, then Nikoly turned to me. "There's going to be a showing of a new designer this evening. They've rented a small museum and it's very private, a guest list of only 200, but we're on it. We'll pick you up at 8."

I used another empty office to check in with Jazz and plow through emails. Nothing had blown up, the story of my fall in Paris had blown over and the fall Santa Anas were blowing in from the desert.

"It's so clear, you can see Catalina." Jazz was jazzed. There was an energy, an electricity in the air when the winds started. Not only did they sweep all the pollution out to sea, but they crackled with potential. One of the potentials was that of wildfires, so Santa Anas were a mixed blessing.

I told her about the event I was attending and promised if any good information came out, I'd get it to her ASAP.

By 7:30, I was ready to meet the oligarchs, or whoever was on that 200-person guest list, so I couldn't put off the next call.

He answered on the first ring. "How is it?" Jean-Louis'

voice made my knees give out and I headed for the sofa, but decided I'd sit in a straight-back desk chair. Kind of like a cold shower.

"It's okay, it's nice, it's, it's different than I expected."

I could feel his smile. "You haven't been to Kiev before, have you? I forget."

"No. I had a quick trip to Moscow once, but never here. It's so modern, and so big!"

"Those are some of the reasons we wanted to put that bureau there. Once the Soviets left, the Ukrainians took off. They want to be seen as a new nation, on the cutting edge of business and technology."

I snickered. "I got that. I met Nikoly and when I asked him what his job was..."

"Did you get the interfacing supply side answer?" By now, Jean-Louis was laughing.

"I did! Did you guys send him to the London School of Economics or something? Or just buy him an MBA?"

Jean-Louis' voice lost its humor. "Don't think he's just an educated jerk. We crammed him full of business-speak when we were planning this expansion to give him a good cover. He's been a family member for about 300 years, so he's seen a lot come and go in the Ukraine. He knows most of the players, maybe not the current heads of clans, but their histories, so he can run a deep background and find out anything."

"That sounds like blackmail!"

"That's exactly what it is. And in that part of the world, it's the business model. Pay to play. The other part is that he knows which of the clans, the thugs, are currently looking for contracts. He'll know who the Huszars are using before they even shake hands. Sandor is going to call him every day."

"Oh, God! I didn't think about phones! This isn't being tapped, is it?"

"No, as long as you use your cell and keep it short. I don't think we need to go to single-use pre-paid phone for you. You're an executive in the largest media conglomerate in the world, and it would look pretty suspicious if you never had the same phone number. Have a good time tonight. Message me if you find anything interesting. I love you."

I managed the business part of the call fine, but started to come apart at that. He could tell my voice was choking up, because he said, "You don't need to message me, I'll be there when you get back from the party."

It didn't matter how or why, Jean-Louis was coming to be with me.

Chapter Seventeen

This was no backward city. Kiev may not get the headlines that other places did, but her people sure read and followed the trends.

The party was at a "small museum" that was originally an 18th century house. The facade was rococo gone tatty but somebody had spent a lot of petrodollars on renovating the inside. It was all steel and glass with cantilevered stories opening up on a central atrium. Taras told me that the roof over the atrium slid open during the summer, but it was closed this night. I know, because through the glass I watched someone's personal helicopter land.

This was money, capital M money. I didn't know the Russian, or Ukrainian, for "trophy wife" but these guys had bought the best of them, then continued to spend. Every Parisian, Milanese and hot New York designer was represented and sables—my God, I hadn't seen this much sable, well, ever—were carelessly slung around shoulders.

The guys looked dumpy, even in their designer suits, and tended to be shorter than the women, not hard considering the women all wore minimum four inch heels. Then they chose to complement their shortish, brutish, hairyish looks with gold. It draped around their wide necks, flowed down their heavy chests, and slipped out to their ham-hock hands in the form of both bracelets and rings.

Like all good A List parties, the place was filled with chatter in a dozen languages and air kisses. Servants toted around trays of iced vodka, so cold it was syrupy, Cristal Champagne, Beluga caviar, tiny blinis with foie gras; everything that was a no-no on a PC foodies list was here. I expected to see sharks' fin or bear's paw or some other Asian delicacy, but this crowd looked west, not east. They knew where their bread had been buttered.

Taras took my arm and steered me to a few of the smaller chatting groups, but the name "SNAP" didn't carry quite the cachet here. These people flaunted their wealth and power in a different way. They had no need to impress the masses, they were out to impress each other and jockey for position in their peer group. I could see we were going to be hard pressed to build a stable of celebrities, but I decided to look at this as a "challenge". I couldn't help smiling when a mental image of Nikoly popped up. Speaking of the vampire, where was he?

I craned around, then took the stairs up to a mezzanine level. The air was cleaner and quieter here—I'd also forgotten that the California no-smoking campaign didn't reach to here. Leaning against the balcony rail, I slipped my right shoe off and stood on the cool stone, easing the pain that standing in stilettos brought. As I closed my eyes and felt the cold stone numbing my toes, a voice in my ear said "Can you be trusted to carry a message?" I jerked around and saw one of the swarthy guests nonchalantly leaning over the rail, watching the crowd.

"Don't react, don't look at me. I'm sending you and your Kandesky masters and pals a message. This is my turf, our turf. Stay out."

By the time I worked up the courage to glance around, he was gone. I couldn't see him on the stairs, and in the crowd below a swarthy short guy in a black suit could have been anybody.

Well, I hadn't been grabbed. Small mercies, I guess. I put my shoe back on and headed back down, only then noticing the small elevator. That was how the guy disappeared so quickly. My deductive powers must have been checked at the door, along with my bodyguard.

Okay, where was everybody? Hadn't Nikoly been on the guest list? And Vladmir had come in the door, leaving Vassily with the driver, but I wasn't seeing them. I was working my way along the edge of the crowd when a hand touched my elbow. I'd learned the hard way what happened when I screamed so I just sucked in—really hard—and turned to see Nikoly.

"I think we'd better leave. I've talked to some people and Taras is still working the room, but I saw that you were approached."

"Approached? Well someone gave me a message." I was whispering in a quavery voice, so I started over. "One of the guests spoke to me, yes." This time it came out a little stronger.

"I've just heard from Jean-Louis and he's landing in about an hour. He'll meet us at the hotel." Nikoly's hand at my waist guided me toward the door, where we picked up Vladmir. It was times like this that the demons weren't so demonic.

Back at our suite, I had time to change before Vassily knocked, Vladmir opened the door and Jean-Louis walked in. I wasn't sure how to act in front of a family member I'd just met. Jean-Louis took the lead. He shook hands with Nikoly and gave me a hug. Nice. Friendly. Nothing more.

"We need to talk about this." He turned to Vladmir. "Go get us some Bull's Blood, some white wine and...what would you like Maxie?"

We were ordering from room service? I wanted a Valium, but doubted that was on the menu. "I'd like some water, please, some Pellegrino?"

Vladmir nodded, spoke into his communicator and headed out the door, reappearing in less than a minute with the order.

Jean-Louis looked at us. "Well?"

I started to sputter when Nikoly stepped in, smooth as satin. "I noticed Maxie on the mezzanine, checking out the crowd, a good move. Then suddenly there was someone beside her. He must have said something, but she was very cool, didn't jump, didn't say anything. He left, she stood there for a few seconds, looked around and headed down the stairs."

That was terse and to the point.

Jean-Louis looked at me. "And your version?"

Not a "Well done", just the facts. Okay.

"I thought maybe I could spot some of the important people better from the balcony, watch who was being surrounded, who people were gravitating to. I saw a few eddys, guests schooling around couples. I was going to ask Taras who they were when this voice said, 'Give your Kandesky pals a message. Stay out of our turf.' I just caught a glimpse of him, he looked like any of the other guests, short, squatty, swarthy, then I closed my eyes and when I opened them, he was gone. I put my shoe on and came downstairs where Nikoly found me."

"You had your shoes off?" Jean-Louis was hard pressed to keep a smile in check.

"No, not my shoes. I just slipped one off for a second."

"Well, if one if the demons isn't near you, taking your shoes off might be good. At least you could run faster."

By now, Nikoly was amused. "Is this something you practice all the time, Maxie?" He had begun a very low glimmer. I thought "Oh, no, not you too" then realized he was just stifling a laugh.

"She's from Southern California." Apparently, Jean-Louis felt this was enough of an explanation. "Nikoly, do you know who this was?"

"I didn't get a good enough look at him. I've put the word out with my watchers and the early consensus is that it was one of the Huszars' shapeshifters. They do have some in this area."

"What Huszars are here now? I thought Matthais had called them home to get ready for an onslaught against us."

Nikoly wrinkled his eyebrows. "Some have gone back to Hungary, but I think Leonid is the highest-ranking Huszar still here. He's fairly high, takes part in Matthais' council meetings and has a pretty free hand."

"What are their moves? We're working with Markov and he's pliant, but not over-long in the brains department. I doubt Matthais brings him in on strategy sessions."

"I agree. Markov is good to have as a soldier, and he will follow leaders and whip up the troops, but subtly...not. My field guys aren't sure, but Leonid seems to be trolling for oligarchs, up-and-coming rich, what passes for the movers and shakers. We're just gathering info and not trying to analyze it yet.

A low hum came from Jean-Louis. "We've heard from others that they're making moves towards civility, so we have watchers, too. One thing that concerns us is that we've heard some regulars are being turned. And not just regulars, some stunning women who could compete with our current celebs."

Now it was Nikoly's turn to frown. "I didn't want to mention that because I thought it was just some isolated cases, but we've had a few here, too. The ones we're watching are turned, then show up on some oligarch's arm, looking like trophy wives. What was that silly American movie a while ago, *Step Wives?*"

"*Stepford Wives.*" Finally, something I could contribute to the conversation. "It was a story about all the men in a town turning their wives into robots. Do you think all the trophy wives are vampires?"

Nikoly and Jean-Louis shared a glance. Jean-Louis stood up and moved to the windows. Kiev at night, a surprisingly urban cityscape, sparkled.

"No, if there was a big increase in the Huszar family, we'd hear about it. Karoly is a member of the council."

He turned back to the room. "It seems odd that this would happen just as we move to get an Eastern bureau up. And the message tonight. Why does our expansion make them nervous, they've never been interested in business or money in the past.

"Well, Nik, let's just keep a close eye on it. Have you and Taras found enough people? Do you have a portfolio we can go over? "

With that, the meeting shifted to *my* ground. When it wrapped up an hour later, I had Jean-Louis all to myself until sunrise, when he'd leave to sleep at Nikoly's home in the suburbs.

We made the best use of the time and when I finally had to sleep because I knew I wouldn't be able to stand up, I laid my head on his beautiful, pale chest and wondered how he could turn me into such a pleasure-seeking, pleasure-needing woman.

Chapter Eighteen

Francois! I'd forgotten about our plans to go to Prague!

Between the incident in Paris, the fast trip to Kiev and the revelation that there seemed to be a bunch of new, beautiful vampires created by the Huszars, Prague was a million years ago.

When I called him to apologize, his breezy voice was a shade more somber.

"I'm so sorry, Francois. I don't usually just blow plans off."

"Not to worry, Maxie. Something has come up here, as well."

"Are you all right?"

"Yes, yes, it's just that one of our paparazzi went missing and when we found him, he'd been threatened."

"That's crazy talk! Who would threaten a paparazzi? With what?"

"Yes, we thought that. He was grabbed by some Slavic type and told he had to follow a couple of young women, then get us to buy the pictures."

I closed my eyes. Now Paris, too? This had to be the Huszars' doing, but what were they doing? I told him that he needed to talk to Jean-Louis immediately then hung up and paced.

Things were heating up. Jean-Louis had said this would be war, but I hadn't seen many signs of if. Well, maybe I didn't know what to look for. I'd always thought that the attacks on me were the only symptom of the struggle, but the Huszars had been hard at work. Turning young woman who could be our camera fodder. Kidnapping and threatening our photographers.

After the meeting at the castle, I had a better picture of what the Kandeskys were planning and understood some ways I could help, but those squat, hairy guys too big for their suits made me nervous. And if they were grabbing one of our paparazzi off the streets of Paris, they could be anywhere.

As my brain was racing like a hamster in a wheel, Vladmir tapped on the door.

"Taras is here. Are you ready?"

Ready? Oh, rats, another thing slipped my mind. We were supposed to go to a reception for the principal Kirov Ballet dancers. Throwing money at the arts was an accepted way for the publicity-shy oligarchs to give and get kudos, so the undercover social schedule was full and Taras had done a great job of making sure SNAP was on all the guest lists. The party-givers were still a little shy of random paparazzi and press coverage, but in a controlled environment, felt comfortable enough to talk to us.

I pulled out a taffeta number—courtesy of Jazz and the Neiman-Marcus shopper—grabbed some heels (take that, Jean-Louis), did a remake of my hair and face and was ready. Even without Elise, I was getting better and faster at this quick-change routine. Tonight was colder so I snatched a fur. It bothered my SoCal anti-fur, PETA sensibilities, but here it was both warmth and camouflage. Without a fur, I would have stood out in this crowd.

I put in a fast call to Jean-Louis and left a message where I was going, when and with whom. And yes, I had my demons with me, both inside and out.

Tonight's gala was a replay of last night. Did these people ever get tired of seeing one another? Well, this wasn't just in Kiev, although the A-list group here was smaller, this closed-circle approach was the same everywhere. And that's how we made money, following around the see-and-be-seen crowd whose membership fluctuated only slightly.

Taras introduced me to several more people, air-kissed some of the women from last night, handed me a flute of Cristel and worked the room like a pro. I talked to two couples, both of whom had "vacation" homes in the U.S. and spoke solid if accented English. They were quietly thrilled that SNAP was going to start coverage of their part of the world, but wouldn't want the constant attention that American celebs or European royalty suffered.

No worries, I wasn't sure that these people would be interesting to the rest of the world.

What was I thinking? Of course they would. Our readers and watchers around the globe would salivate at an interview with someone who paid $100 million for a house! These were probably the anonymous bidders who paid six and seven figure prices at Sotheby's for paintings and object d'arts. My time with the Kandeskys had dulled my edge. Now I was one of the people we covered. I wore those designer gowns. I rode in limos. I had bodyguards.

I mentally slapped myself and was shifting back to coverage mode when a sudden current ran through the crowd. People edged away from the door and I could see a man coming into the room. He was not terribly tall, just under 6 feet, had a shock of white hair, glacier-blue eyes and wore a beautifully-cut dinner suit. But he was also the whitest person I'd ever seen. No, not white, translucent. If he'd had any blood, you would have seen it coursing through his veins. The man next to me whispered "Leonid!"

So, this was the resident Huszar. He was followed by an entourage. Three pale, pale women dressed in varying shades of red with sables trailing on the floor and two bodyguards, shortish, darkish, largish men, poured into their suits. Slavs? Chechens? Shapeshifters? It didn't matter, they were trouble.

As he came across the floor, the crowd fell back so that, by the time he reached me, we were isolated, as separate as if we were the spotlight dance.

He smiled, not showing his fangs, and said, "Hello, you're Maxmillia Gwenoch. I am Leonid."

A sigh went through the guests, as though they all let their breath out at once.

Leonid turned to the women. "Let me introduce you. This is Natasha, Anna and Olga. Say hello to Ms. Gwenoch from SNAP, girls."

The "girls" all nodded; their "hellos" were indistinguishable.

"We heard you are looking for some new talent for your enterprise here." Leonid had a slight lisp. "We wanted to make sure that our girls were among the contenders. Didn't we, girls?" He turned to them and they nodded again.

This was just too weird. Did Leonid lisp because he'd spent years, centuries hissing at his prey? Were the "girls" regulars, donors, or were they women who'd been turned by the Huszars?

I was so astounded by Leonid and his circus that I didn't see Jean-Louis and Nikoly, but suddenly Jean-Louis' voice filled the silence.

"Hello, Leonid, I thought you'd been recalled. Isn't Matthais looking for you?"

Now the crowd sucked in a breath. Wow, what was going on here? Did everybody know that these were vampires? And from rival families?

"Well, Jean-Louis, and I see you have Nikoly with you. Did the Baron let you out to play?"

Nikoly's silky voice cut in. "Leonid, this is a festive event. We've all come to meet and welcome the wonderful dancers from Kirov. Let's, for tonight, put on our civilized manners. Who are these lovely ladies?" and he turned to the "girls". They became more animated with another vamp, so I decided they were probably donors, vampire wanna-be's, roadies. They all smiled, not enough to see fangs if they were there, and introduced themselves.

Tension eased and the sound level rose as people started chewing over the scene they'd just seen. They darted glances towards us, maybe hoping for some more fireworks?

Jean-Louis took my arm. "Shall we go?" He started to make a path through the crowd but I pulled my arm away.

"I need to find Taras. He was going to introduce me to more people."

Sudden chill. Oops, I guess that wasn't a suggestion. My mother always told me *"Ladies don't make scenes. They wait until they're in private to stab someone."* Wait until I get this man in private!

"Taras will be told we had to leave. He can call you tomorrow."

Well, OK, then. I headed towards the door, leaving Jean-Louis to trail along behind me. It was good for SNAP that neither of us wanted a public showdown

Vladmir opened the door to the waiting limo, Jean-Louis practically pushed me in then fell on top of me, Vladmir crammed himself into the front seat and we all but peeled out of there. I was slammed back again the seat and fumbling for my seatbelt when Jean-Louis gave an order in Hungarian. He turned to me, said "Don't bother with that, just get on the floor" and shoved my head down as the limo made a sharp right. All I could see from the floor was dark, no streetlights, just looming buildings. We made a sudden left, the brakes squealed and we plowed to a stop.

Jean-Louis was using Vladmir's communicator, Vassily and the driver were checking the magazines in their Sig Sauers and Vladmir was coiling some fine, thin wire that glowed. I took Jean-Louis' order and tucked myself further into the floor well, wrapping my head in my arms and trying to stop the sudden shaking.

What was going on? Jean-Louis, Nikoly and Leonid were talking in veiled threats, but it hadn't sounded like an overt declaration. Vampire-speak wasn't a language I read well. It seemed I missed a lot of undertone. Then things happened.

I couldn't see, but I could hear the communicating window sliding up, car doors slamming open and deep, powerful animal growls. I was alone, cocooned in the back of the armored limo, trapped but safe.

I heard some muted pops, not even as loud as a kid's BB gun, some wordless yelling and a strange snaky, hissing sound. The limo rocked as heavy rounds hit it, but nothing penetrated my cave and gradually the shots stopped.

There was a minute of quiet, then a powerful engine started and the limo was sideswiped with a ripping, crunching blow that sounded like the inside of a steel mill, all screeching, tearing metal lit by showers of sparks that seared my eyelids. Then only the sound of a large vehicle leaving.

Was I trapped for good in a demolished car? Were the demons dead? Where was Jean-Louis?

Chapter Nineteen

The hand that ripped the crushed door open belonged to somebody very, *very* strong. So strong that I wasn't about to look. If the Huszars had me, well, I'd just as soon not know until I had to.

Then the hand took my arm in a grip I knew would leave bruises and an accented voice said, "Are you alright?"

Vladmir. It was Vladmir grabbing me, then reaching in and lifting me from the cave that had become a death trap.

Once out and being carried by him, there was enough moonlight that I could see we'd ended up in a dead-end lot criss-crossed by unused rail sidings, meaning this had been the heart of factories during Kiev's earlier heyday. It also meant that nobody was around.

Vladmir set me down. My gown was in sad shape from my cowering on the floor and I was barefoot. He reached back into the wreck and rummaged around until he found my fur, wrapping it around me to slow the shivering. He handed me my shoes with a shrug and I saw that the strap on one broke off. Well, at least the soles would keep my feet off the asphalt that was littered with glass, nails, bits of sharp metal and loads of tetanus germs.

"Where's Jean-Louis?" I managed, my jaw clenching from cold and fear.

"He and Nikoly are following Leonid."

"I didn't even see another car. Are they hurt?"

"I can't tell you. Jean-Louis will tell you when they come back. Come, sit in the front seat, it's not so damaged."

And so I sat in the front seat of a smashed limo in an abandoned factory yard of a former Soviet Republic in the cold and dark. I'd really come far in my career.

Vladmir's communicator crackled, he answered in a rush of Hungarian and turned to me. "Jean-Louis is on his way back."

He was alive. That meant I could yell at him for not telling me what was going on.

Another Mercedes limo pulled up, this one white but still driven by a demon, and Nikoly and Jean-Louis got out. My anger melted away as I saw Nikoly's left arm hanging, almost swinging free, and his suit and shirt streaked with blood.

"What happened?" I was stammering.

"You probably heard most of it." Jean-Louis sounded tired, wrung out with the hangover of adrenaline. "I knew they were following us, planning an attack. I didn't think they'd try ramming us. That's why we went after them. That's a new tactic and I want to find out when they learned it. But now," he turned to Nikoly, "we have to get him home and have someone look at him. I think he has silver poisoning as well as the wound. Come on."

He got me in the back, Vladmir in the front, gave brief instructions to the demon driving and we headed out of town. At the house, a largish estate in the outskirts, the door was opened by a demon who picked Nikoly up and took him off to get tended to.

"I need to know all that happened, but first I'd like a glass of wine." Jean-Louis nodded and led me into a sitting room, motioning at a servant, who came back shortly with a tray and glasses.

He waved the demon away and poured white wine for me and Bull's Blood for himself.

"When I saw Leonid talking to you, with those women in tow, I knew he was pushing the envelope. My suspicion is that he thinks he can gain control over you if most of the talent and celebs we feature are his creatures. If he provides the content, he'll be able to manipulate you."

"Who were those women? They acted like they'd been drugged."

"We think they're donors. At least they start out as donors. And they're probably drugged. The word we've heard is that the Huszars are recruiting young women with the promise that if they're chosen, they'll have eternal life and eternal fame. Well, for the ones they turn, yes, eternal life. But fame? No. Once they get turned, they'll find out what the Huszars really are. They'll be no more than slaves. And of course, as we've found out, you can't have eternal fame. Somebody will remember you and wonder why you haven't aged. And all of that is the beginning step of their attempt to take us over."

Even with the background I'd learned, I hadn't jumped to the conclusion that they wanted to take over the Kandeskys. The Baron and family were just too entrenched, too educated, too sophisticated.

"You hadn't thought that far." I got a faint lift at the corners of his mouth and his eyes lost some of the haunted look.

Damn, would I never be able to keep my thoughts and emotions under check so these vampires couldn't read me?

"No, I hadn't. I thought they just wanted me so they could compete. When you said 'war' I didn't think it meant to the end of us all."

He laid back in the chair and stretched his legs out. It wasn't late, but he'd, we'd, had a lot tonight. I was close to exhaustion, and he was showing signs of weariness. I went over to him and touched his arm. He grabbed me around the waist, pulled me into his lap and buried his face in my hair.

"You are so soft," he said against my ear. "When you first started, when all this business with the Huszars started, I thought I could just handle this with diplomacy, talk, maybe a few bribes. The game changed so fast, I'm not keeping up. And now, because of you, I'm afraid of losing more, so I can't show how vulnerable I am."

A knock at the door, Jean-Louis said, "Come," and a middle-aged man with a doctor's coat over his suit came in with Vladmir tagging behind.

"It's not the best, but he'll come through it." The man

scrubbed a hand over his face. Was he a vampire or a regular? Was this the middle of the night or the middle of his day? Whichever, he looked exhausted, too.

"What's the damage?"

The doctor sat down. "The wound is nasty, but it'll heal. It looks like the bone is already starting to knit."

"The bones are broken?"

"Yes. The bullet broke the humerus below the shoulder socket. The head wasn't smashed, so even with chips, it's still clean. The muscles are ripped up, but nothing's missing. The problem is the silver."

The room was silent. I knew the Kandeskys and their demons used silver ammunition. Of course, the Huszars did too. Now I was seeing firsthand what that really meant. I'd just thought of it as "special" ammunition that killed. Now I realized it poisoned as well.

Jean-Louis took a sip from his glass. "Will he survive?"

"Yes. It'll take time for him to overcome it. The best thing is for him to have complete rest and a safe place."

"Thank you doctor. Vladmir will see you home. You won't speak of this to anyone."

"No, I understand the implications. No one in Kiev knows that I serve as a back-up physician to the Kandeskys, and as a regular, I intend to keep it that way. It's much better for my health." He stood, shook Jean-Louis' hand and left. Never spoke to me. Never even saw me.

Just as well, after what I'd seen tonight.

"Tell me what you did to the Huszars." I needed to know that they had as much damage as we did. We. I realized I was thinking and acting as one of the family. Odd.

"It was a mixed group. Leonid, of course, and two of his shapeshifters. And they had three Chechens, as well, acting as drivers and guards. I know we shot, and killed, I think, two of the Chechens. One of the shapeshifters is dead. We managed to get Leonid immobilized with the silver wire."

Ahh, that must have been the snaky sound I heard.

"They were driving an armored SUV, like the ones the Secret Service in the U.S. uses. They're big, heavy vehicles with a higher profile than our Mercedes, so when the last Chechen got Leonid into the car, he decided to ram us. If I hadn't gotten you down into the floor well, you would have been hurt. The Mercedes has heavier armor down the sides and across the bottom as protection against roadside bombs. I was worried they had rocket grenades."

Roadside bombs? Rocket grenades? This may have been a former Soviet country, but it wasn't the Middle East.

"Do you guys, you vampires, have rocket grenades?" I knew my voice was up in the soprano range. "Don't you just rely on...I don't know, regular weapons and speed and strength and..." I ran out of words.

Jean-Louis pulled out the patience he'd use for a small child. "Generally, we do. But this is the former Eastern bloc and they're still finding their way. The rulers are the strong men. That translates to thugs with money. And thugs with money find the most up-to-date weapons."

"I thought you just needed silver bullets and wire." Guns, violence, were way out of my comfort range. I'd learned to ignore the bulges under the demon's jackets

"Those are personnel weapons, fine if we have them, or they have us, in the open. When we're traveling, conventional weapons are best. Blow up the car we're in *then* use the silver."

That made sense. I'd been traveling around in the Baron's fleet of armored Mercedes and didn't think through all the implications. Now, every time I got into one, the memories would come flooding back.

I must have grunted because his hooded, dark eyes softened. "It's been eventful and you looked whacked. You'll stay here tonight. We can defend the house. Vladmir will pack up your hotel room and tomorrow we're going home."

One of Nikoly's demons picked me up and, with Jean-Louis trailing behind, took me to a bedroom already made up. Jean-Louis held me until I fell asleep, which took probably all of five minutes.

Chapter Twenty

They'd held dinner for us at the castle. We pulled up and walked straight into the dining room where the Baron, Pen and Bela were already seated. As Jean-Louis and I took our seats, the meal, more casual and hurried than usual, was served, eaten and cleared away.

Then came the night's discussion, but this time instead of being just the agenda, I was given a voice.

"We didn't expect that Leonid was so tight with the Chechens." Jean-Louis began the story of Kiev. "We were watching Maxie, and Nikoly and his demons were on the alert. Taras only knows that a possible rival has hired some Chechen thugs to make it uncomfortable. He thinks we might sell out if we're too bothered, and we want to keep him thinking that way. Just a routine business squabble with the oligarchs looks good."

He was twiddling with his napkin and looked up with a wry grin. "It's a good thing we're not a publicly-traded company."

The tension eased some as Pen and the Baron laughed gently, but Bela seemed mystified, so Jean-Louis took a side trip down the fast lane of explanation about hostile takeovers and stockholder revolts.

"Thank Nikoly for us," the Baron said. "I think we should bring him here to recuperate."

"I mentioned it. As soon as the bone heals, I'm sending the plane for him. Silver poisoning can be tricky and we know the best ways to counteract it. We'll make sure that Taras spreads the word that Nikoly is going to the Caribbean for relaxation after his run-in with the Chechens."

He turned to me. "You need to be the one who tells

Taras what Nikoly's plans are. That will help solidify your standing in SNAP management and pull attention away from the family."

The others nodded and I was obscurely pleased that I'd been accepted.

This could be a two-edged sword, though. While I was happy that I was finally part of the family, it also made me stick up more as a lightning rod for all the baddies. My mother's voice drifted through my head, *"If you stand out from the crowd, you're likely to be shot at."*

The discussion continued most of the night. There was agreement that we keep on with the plans for building up the Kiev bureau. Jean-Louis and I talked about the Huszar's attempt to lure young women with the promise of everlasting life, and what that might mean to our finding true celebs to follow.

One of my tasks was to have Francois get in touch with all the fashion houses and alert them that we were searching for Eastern Europeans. The oligarchs were so private that finding them was difficult, so finding their shopping patterns was next best.

Jean-Louis was continuing to meet with Karoly and Alessandr who were quietly talking to Huszar family members about their dissatisfaction. Matthais' violent leadership was fine during the wars, and helped the family weather the hardships during the Communist era, but now that money was flowing and people traveling, they were itching to get a piece of the action.

And for them, that didn't mean just going out on nighttime raids for food. They saw the glitz and glamour and wanted in on the goodies of fame, fast cars, beautiful women and expensive clothes. Some of the younger members of the Huszar family were 300 years old, but having been turned at 18 or 23 or whatever, in their prime as young adults, they still had testosterone raging. That made them good soldiers for Matthais. And it made them lust for more of the material things of the regular world, mostly revolving around women.

The Baron, Bela and Jean-Louis groaned. "That's one of the reasons we don't take many young people as acolytes," Jean-Louis said. "Chasing after women gets in the way of business. They're also more unstable and make the family vulnerable to scrutiny."

He had the grace to let a small grin cross his face. That was one of the reasons the Kandesky elders were upset at Jean-Louis when he started showing an interest in me. Most of them had been in stable relationships for centuries and to have the second in command get seriously involved with a regular—a regular on their payroll and an executive in their business—could bring a lot of scrutiny.

Those pitfalls didn't hamper the Huszars. Money could buy them entree into the echelons of attractiveness. Money could buy them bait for women—jewelry, fast cars, travel, luxury—even though many of those women always had an eye out for the richer, older, sexier men. Of course, the Huszars had one thing that trumped all the money and power—eternal life. Using money and all the trappings lured some young women, and the hook was set with the lifetime guarantee.

What they didn't see, and what the Huszars didn't tell them, was that they couldn't trade on their youth and beauty forever. They still had to be seen in the regular world and people would talk when they never aged. So they bought an eternal life where they gave up the pleasures of being seen and admired in the regular world, for a world that only admired them as a lure for others.

As Jean-Louis ran down our assessment of the Huszars, Pen nodded in agreement. She had been one of the world's leading celebrities, not an actress, not an aristocrat, just a beautiful, cultured woman admired for years for her panache and elegance. The time had come a few months before when the Kandeskys bowed to the inevitable.

Pen had been a star in the celebrity world for better than 40 years and tongues were wagging about lots of surgery; it was time for her to retire. In today's digital world of 24/7 news cycles, instant communications, cloud computing, images never went away and even in a century, some sharp-eyed photographer or editor might recognize her if she were to re-emerge as a celeb.

"We have so much more than the Huszars." The Baron waved his hand around. "Not just material things, although we have a lot more of that, but interests, businesses, influence. We move in spheres that the Huszars have never conceived. It would be incredibly dangerous to allow them money and power. They supported Hitler because it helped them out. They have no understanding or caring about the way the world folds in on itself. How one action can have severe consequences, not only to them but to others. Can you imagine if they aligned themselves with one of today's rogue states?"

Everyone murmured. We all understood the potential chaos that could be unleashed. The Huszars had to be reined in and controlled, our only discussion was about finding the best way to do that.

I was beginning to droop and still hadn't taken Jean-Louis to task over scaring the hell out of me when I thought he'd been killed. He felt my emotions and stood. "I'm taking Maxie to bed; she's probably on the edge of shock."

Wait a minute. I wasn't a child, to be put to bed! I started a snide comment then bit my tongue as a combination of fatigue and desire swept over me. I was tired. I wanted Jean-Louis. Comforting me while I fell asleep was fine and all, but I wanted this beautiful man to make love to me. I wanted his hands to undress me. I wanted his lovely, naked body next to me and I wanted him to make me forget.

Chapter Twenty-one

We were engulfed in a whirl of activity the next few days. Jazz and I had two or three Skype conversations a day, I talked with Francois, Taras and Carola about the upcoming holidays, I had to work out coverage assignments for the spring fashion shows and always, wonderfully, magically there was Jean-Louis.

I felt at the top of my game, with an enthusiasm and energy I hadn't had since my first months with SNAP, when I was making a name and creating my persona. All those self-doubts were gone. Without that nagging sense that I was in over my head, I just let things roll off me instead of hunting for hidden messages.

These few days were a respite from the tension with the Huszars, and Jean-Louis was able to spend a few hours with me every night. It's wasn't just the sex that was making me want more of him—although it was glorious. This man clearly had years of experience with women and my skin tingled when he touched me, knowing what was to come.

Best part though, was that he was letting me know him. He told me stories of his turning and how difficult it was for him at first as an acolyte of the Baron. How hard it was for him to learn to feed and not always kill. How traumatic to find an attractive woman and know that he couldn't have her forever. How he hardened himself to short relationships and tamped down the qualms about using women.

But he didn't tell me about Magda. His wife. His one love.

He had casually asked me if I would let him feed off me, but when I cringed, he backed away. I was falling more in love with this stunning creature, but I couldn't give my life completely over to him.

"I won't ever push you to become my donor. I have plenty of food and you're too precious to me to frighten away," he whispered to me one night as he was stroking me. My legs fell open and I wanted to take all of him into me but I wasn't able to let him pierce my skin.

I knew this idyll wouldn't last, if for no other reason than my legs wouldn't hold me up after he left to go to his own rooms.

And I was right.

One night, the Baron summoned all of us to the media room. He had CNN on one screen, Al Jazeera on another and BBC on a third. All of them were reporting on an overnight attack on an Afghan town that left 25 dead. What was so different about this attack was that no one was taking credit for it. No Taliban communiqués, no Al Qaeda statements, no traces of car bombs or other incendiary devices. What witnesses they could find reported some shots, but most of them only saw black-robed figures going into the victims' homes.

After a few minutes of watching the news tapes loop, the Baron muted the televisions. "Well, what's your best guess?" He turned to us but was really addressing Jean-Louis.

"It doesn't take a genius to know this one." Jean-Louis was pacing, running his hands through his hair. "This has Huszar written all over it, and the Taliban and Al Qaeda are trying to keep their distance. I knew it was going to be a bloodbath if they got mixed up with the rogues in the area."

I just sat there, open-mouthed. "Why would terrorist groups want to hook up with the Huszars? They don't have the same aims. They don't care about Islam. They don't hate the West.

"Or do they?" I turned to Jean-Louis, then the Baron, looking for some answers because this didn't make sense.

"No, the Huszars don't have those aims. Their aim is to gain power, control and money. This looks like a product sample. Showing off a new weapons system to a potential buyer." The Baron shook his head and hit the remote button, sending the newscasters into the void. "I, we, were afraid that something like this might happen. Once they contacted with the Chechens to do some of their daylight work, it's a small step to contracting with all those thugs for nighttime work. The one saving grace is that they are the weapons themselves, so they can only do limited damage.

"But what a handy addition to have. I doubt that Al Qaeda, or whomever, is paying them very much. A little cash, you provide the food and bingo, the Huszars stage a raid and scare the populace into toeing the line."

I shuddered. All those poor people in the Middle East and Eastern Europe. Centuries of warfare, shifting tribal alliances, and now modern warfare, terrorists and vampires at large. What did they ever do to deserve this?

The Baron turned to Jean-Louis. "Take Sandor and a couple of demons. Go pick up Bela. Meet Karoly at the tunnel in the Neutrality and bring him in. We need to talk."

Jean-Louis nodded and headed for the armory and all I could do was sit there making fish-faces with my mouth. I finally got my body to move and ran to the armory myself.

"Take me with you," I begged as the demons loaded up Sig Sauers and filled magazines. Jean-Louis turned to me, astounded. "Are you kidding? You're what most of the Huszar energy is focused on."

"But they must have taken me off the agenda, if they're putting themselves up as murder for hire with terrorists!"

"Don't bet on it." Jean Louis pulled on a pair of surgical gloves, picked up a coil of silver wire and handed it to one of the demons. "This is just an aside. They can't make the money from these idiots that they can from you. Plus, hanging out with thugs, terrorists, rogue states, doesn't get them the panache they want in the West. Even if they make a lot of money, they can't flaunt it. They'd never make the A-list, probably not even in Kiev."

"I still want to go. Maybe even more, if I'm still a target. I don't want to be cowering behind some demon while you're out there getting yourself killed!" My voice started to quaver.

That made him stop. "Are you worried that I might get killed?"

"Of course I am. Most of what you thought was an adrenaline hangover in Kiev was residual fear about you. If you get killed, I don't want to be here any more."

"Hummm, that's sounding awfully like a suicide wish. I still won't let you commit suicide, though."

I stomped my foot and the gesture startled me. I hadn't stomped my foot since I was five and my crummy sister wouldn't give me my doll. "It's not suicide, you big doofus, it's the opposite. I worry less if I know what's going on than I do if I have to *guess* what's going on. It's much scarier to sit and wait for news."

He sighed. He sighed again and slapped the gloves on his leg. He sighed again and rolled his eyes at the demons, but they didn't respond. Clearly, they weren't picking sides in this lose-lose proposition.

He paced around the armory, ostensibly looking for weapons, but really looking for an answer that would shut me up. He didn't find one.

He sighed. "All right. But, we're only going to the end of the tunnel. We're not going into the Neutrality. We're just going to meet Karoly and bring him back. You can carry a knife and some wire. Two demons will be in front of you and one behind. Don't get away from them. Oh, I hope I'm not going to be sorry."

I looked up at him. Now that I was going, I was scared to death, but I meant what I'd said. No matter how scared, it was better than the stress of waiting to hear that he was dead. "You won't be sorry, my love." There, I'd said it in front of the demons. No matter how much I wanted to hold him now, that show of emotion wasn't done.

There was a small door in a niche in the armory and as we headed through it and down a flight of narrow stairs, I was glad that I'd been SoCal dressed when Jean-Louis and I were in my apartment, before the summons from the Baron. I had on jeans and a shirt and grabbed a tailored leather jacket and a pair of soft-soled shoes as we'd headed out. Most of the time, I was barefoot in my own rooms, a California holdover that made Jean-Louis crazy, but, hey, we all had our idiosyncrasies.

He was a vampire and drank blood; I went barefoot.

Chapter Twenty-two

The staircase was some twenty steps down and then leveled off to a floor that sloped slightly downward. It was carved out of the stone heart of the mountains and lined with more paving stones. Although the air was damp and smelled old, the tunnel was dry.

Sconces every few feet lined the walls, for the days when the world was lit only by fire. This was now, though, and the tunnel was wired for electricity in addition to the heavy, powerful flashlights carried by a couple of the demons. When I looked closely at the flashlights, I realized they had heavy silver switches and belt hooks and doubled as weapons.

We didn't make much noise. Jean-Louis had made sure none of us jingled. All weapons were holstered or otherwise secured and we all wore silent shoes. He'd told me that he didn't think the Huszars knew about the tunnel, but none of the Kandeskys took any chances.

The shapeshifters roaming the Neutrality above us had keen hearing and the night birds, particularly the owls who called these woods their own, could hear a mole in its den. The owls weren't part of the Huszars, but when an owl alerted to some sound, the shapeshifters, usually werewolves, paid attention.

We walked, silently but quickly, for what felt like twenty minutes when I realized the floor was now slightly sloping up. After another five minutes, we came to a second set of stairs, leading up into a well of darkness. Sandor motioned us to stay at the bottom, the lights and flashlights were snapped off, and he headed up. When he got to the top, I could hear a creaky sound, like an unoiled door opening, a breeze of fresh air trickled in and the darkness wasn't quite so dark.

Jean-Louis headed up, followed by another demon. I was itching to go up those stairs, so when Sandor and Jean-Louis were no longer at the top, I climbed up. I got to the top and stuck my head out just as a crashing, smashing sound came tearing through the underbrush. Yelps and brutish grunts echoed off the trees, but no voices...and no trace of Sandor or Jean-Louis. I started to climb out when something grabbed my leg from behind and dragged me down, not caring if I hit the steps or not, and a hand slapped across my mouth.

I hit the stones at the bottom of the stairs so hard I was winded. Then I felt, I don't think I consciously heard, a demon. "Do not say a word. Do not make a sound. There is danger."

So I huddled at the foot of the stairs, unable to see in the pitch black, hearing only crashes from above and, once again, not knowing if Jean-Louis was dead or alive—or captured by the Huszars.

Some minutes later, the creak sounded again, feet quickly and quietly rushed down the stairs and a demon said "Let's go". I was unceremoniously picked up and carried, fast enough that I felt air flying by, and suddenly we were at the other set of stairs. The flashlights flicked back on and I saw Sandor, demons, Jean-Louis, Karoly and someone I didn't know.

An unseen hand pulled a well-oiled door open and light from the Baron's armory flooded the top of the stairs. We climbed up and out, again Sandor in the lead, and now I got my first good look at the newcomer. He looked faintly Asian, maybe Slavic, with wide-set black eyes in a darkish face; taller and slimmer than the other Slavs I met in Kiev.

His hand, when he reached out to shake mine, was finer-boned and his skin cool. I got the impression that he stopped himself from clicking his heels together and bowing. "Hello, I am Bohdan, from Ukraine. You must be Miss Maxie. I have heard much about you."

Wow, he had more manners that all the other Huszars put together. I'd have to ask Jean-Louis about him.

I nodded, he smiled, Jean-Louis waved his hand in a "wagons, ho!" gesture and we were herded back into the media room, where Pen, the Baron, Milos and two Kandeskys I didn't know were chatting while the talking heads on the TV sets silently mouthed the day's horrors.

"Welcome Karoly." The Baron indicated some chairs. "And I see you've brought Bohdan. How are you old friend? I don't see much of you these days."

"No sir. Leonid is watching me. I even participate in the attack on Miss Maxie and Jean-Louis in Kiev to divert any suspicion."

Bohdan may have come from a mannered background, but English wasn't his first, second or probably even third language. The Baron switched to what I thought was Russian and one of the demons leaned over to translate for me.

It seemed that Matthais was getting frustrated at his attempts to kidnap me, so he starting branching out. Opening our SNAP bureau in Kiev gave him an opportunity to orchestrate a grab and blame the Chechens or some other Mafia-style group. When Jean-Louis and Nikoly managed to deflect the grab, Matthias thought, correctly, that he had a mole in his Kiev staff. He recalled some of the Huszars and Bohdan was now right where the Kandeskys wanted him, just across the Neutrality.

A translator whispering in my ear lost some of the nuances, but the gist was that the Kandeskys were mounting a big disinformation blitz. They moved up the inaugural broadcast from Kiev, and ran clips of me at the parties for the Kirov Ballet. They also shot a party for the daughter of the Azerbaijan president, an incredibly lavish affair paid for by the Baku oil money, and cobbled together a story introducing the new celebs.

Of course this was new, even if the parties were several days earlier, because no one had seen them before. And for damn sure the Azerbaijians, Ukrainians and other oil-soaked oligarchs on the edges of the Caspian Sea didn't want their faces in the media. They were media-smart enough to not complain, but a lot of the footage was the back of swarthy men and beautiful women holding their hands in front of their faces.

No matter, we had a great voice-over, giving a short history of the area, an estimate of the petrodollars flowing into the countries, long shots of the gorgeous women shopping on Rodeo Drive and Boul'St. Germaine and miles of tinted-window limos.

Upshot was, the Kiev bureau was up and running, I was back in the States and Bohdan was off the hook for letting me get away.

Now came the strategy. Bohdan was all for bringing in more and more of the disaffected younger Huszar acolytes.

"We're tired to live in Dark Ages. We see what lifes the rich peoples live. We want to live that way. Hunting, killing, all the violence is not good way to live. We need to be friends, colleagues with our neighbors, with Kandeskys. You help us find the right way, please." Bohdan struggled through this short speech in English, I guess wanting to make sure I understood how deep his feelings were.

In Hungarian, Karoly brought the Baron and Jean-Louis up to date on Matthais' latest orders. It seemed the head of the Huszar family was succumbing to a form of megalomania, ordering his vampires to further and further depredations.

If the younger family members wanted more money, well Matthais would find a way to bring some in. He had a commodity that he could charge for—murder squads. Their kind of killing didn't leave any forensic traces. There wasn't a big outlay for weaponry. Movement across international borders was easy and efficient because the vampires didn't recognize borders. And it all happened at night, when there were fewer nosy witnesses.

"You're right, Baron, the raid in Afghanistan was a sales pitch. Matthais figured if the squad could make it work there, with all the troops around, it would work anywhere. And it was a big success. He's already getting orders in from other places in the Middle East and Africa." Karoly sat back, his hand across his eyes. "It will never be a big scale weapon, there just aren't enough of us...them. It does terrify people, though. We, vampires, are the stuff that nightmares are made of. This is right down the terrorist's alley."

He turned to me. "Don't think that you're off the hook. This little business is just a sideline. There's never going to be enough money in it. He's still zeroing in on you as his ticket to the international big time."

Karoly's eyes swept the table. "And Baron, Pen, Jean-Louis, you know that Matthais' ultimate goal is to eliminate you and all your family."

Jean-Louis looked grim. His eyes were black and flat, reflecting no light, he was translucent and his skin just draped over his skull like thin silk. "Yes, I know. And I know why."

Chapter Twenty-three

The room was so still I could hear my heart pounding.

It must have been loud because Jean-Louis looked at me and raised an eyebrow. I shrugged back. I know that the sound of hearts pumping blood through a regular's cardiovascular system was a dangerous attraction to vampires, so I willed myself to be silent.

Willing my heart to slow though, didn't even put a parking brake on my mind. It was racing in circles, getting me nowhere.

What did he know? Whatever it was, it was enough for Matthais to want to wipe out the entire Kandesky family. He was willing to declare war, and kill off much of his own family to win.

Jean-Louis stood. "That's land I don't want to plow tonight. He and I and the Baron know what hatred Matthais bears us. We will have to solve that another night. It is not a secret I can share, and has no bearing on what we must do to stop him from his current madness.

"Come, Sandor and I will accompany you back."

This time I didn't beg to go. I'd had enough of that tunnel and, frankly, Jean-Louis scared me when he was in this state.

I headed up to my apartment. To wait. To worry until I heard him at my door, safe again.

I couldn't go to bed until I knew, so I curled up by the fireplace with a new mystery that Jazz had sent. Something, some noise was working its way into the plot of the mystery and I knew it didn't belong. Like an old theater when somebody mixed up the movie reels. Growls, low-pitched snarls? In a New York high-rise?

I dropped the book and bolted out of the chair. No! Those were noises coming from outside, and coming louder and faster! Elise came running in just as the door opened. A demon said, "Turn out the light. Get away from the window."

Well, of course I was going to obey a demon when Jean-Louis was still somewhere out there. I did use a little stealth. I eased the edge of a curtain back just as the outside lights blazed on. It was the pigs, they'd banded together and caught a demon in the Neutrality. He was strong and he was fast, but there were about a dozen of the feral boars chasing him. One of them had managed to gore the demon's thigh which was streaming blood that looked black in the intense light.

The others in the band went into blood-lust at the smell and attacked and attacked, screaming in ear-piercing fury. The demon was putting up a good fight. He wrestled his gun out and shot, killing one pig, but they just charged and overwhelmed him, gouging with their tusks and pounding with their sharp hooves.

One hooked his arm and his gun went flying, followed by his arm, torn off his body.

This whole scene wasn't more that a few seconds long, because half-a-dozen demons flooded the terrace, shooting pigs left and right. Four of the pigs fell and the rest fled into the woods, demons in pursuit.

I couldn't look at what was left on the manicured front lawn. It didn't resemble a body, just blood, bones and tissue strewn about. Two house demons came down with a tarp and body bag, but from what I'd seen, there wasn't enough to put in the bag.

Elise pulled me away from the window. "I'm turning the lamps back on. Can I make you some tea?"

"Thank you, yes"

It would take more than a cup of tea to erase what was seared into my retinas. Tonight was a sleeping pill night.

No, no it wasn't! Where was Jean-Louis? If the pigs found that demon in the Neutrality, he might have been part of

Jean-Louis' escort party for Karoly and Bohdan. No sleep, no rest, until I knew.

I pulled on the jeans and shirt I'd worn earlier, crammed my feet into flip-flops—let their well-bred eyes stare—and jammed down the stairs. And discovered why you didn't want to run down marble floors in flip-flops. Luckily, I didn't fall until I hit the bottom of the stairs, but when I turned toward the front of the castle, where the armory was, my foot slid sideways, the thong between my toes ripped out and my ankle hit the marble just seconds before my whole body landed on it.

Oh, fudge, that hurt. I screamed. I screamed "Fudge!" It wasn't quite as satisfying, but it did bring help.

Sandor appeared and lifted me into a chair. Another demon ran to get ice. And Jean-Louis, oh God, it was Jean-Louis, was kneeling, my ankle in his beautiful hands, probing for broken bones.

That's when I couldn't hold back the tears.

"Hush, hush. It will be all right. I don't think any bones are broken. The doctor will check you."

Jean-Louis waved the demon aside and carried me himself. Then I noticed the blood.

"You're hurt!"

"Huummff."

"What happened? Why is your shirt bloody?"

"Hush, don't worry."

"Don't worry!" I squirmed around to see better and almost ended up back on the hard marble. "You come in all bloody and say 'Don't worry!'? "

"Stop squirming and be quiet! I almost dropped you. It's not my blood."

Ahhh. I kept my calm until he laid me on my bed. Elise was fussing slightly, her mouth tight in her pale face. She fluffed pillows up behind me, threw a light cover over me and went to get another cup of tea. She wasn't happy, but I didn't know whether it was me or the pigs or Jean-Louis who had displeased her.

The doctor came in, probed around in the same spots Jean-Louis had, pronounced a nasty sprain, wrapped it, ordered more ice, left me a pain pill and went back to bed. He'd come to stay for a couple of days while Nikoly was healing and clearly wanted to get back to his routine—life at the castle had more drama than he wanted.

So there I lay, in my bed with Jean-Louis pacing around.

"What happened? If that's not your blood, whose is it?" The pain pill was kicking in and I was hard-pressed to keep up a head of anger.

"It's Sandor's."

"Sandor's! Oh no, was he the demon that the pigs tore apart?" This was terrible news. You don't get friendly with demons, they're just too reserved, but Sandor was with me a lot. I'd come to rely on him and trust him. I'd almost seen him smile!

"No, that was Jancek. He was a good soldier, but not as quick as some."

"Back up. Start at the beginning. I saw you and Sandor leave the media room with Karoly and Bohdan..."

"Yes. We picked up Vladmir and Jancek. When we got to the end of the tunnel, Sandor checked. Everything seemed still so the two Huszars slipped away. We were just heading back into the tunnel when an owl caught Sandor's arm with a talon. Sandor tore his arm away and grunted. That was enough to alert a band of hunting pigs who screamed and charged. Jancek started running towards the castle and the pigs followed. I don't know if he thought he could outrun them, or he did it as a decoy, to let the rest of us get safely away."

I thought about the demon I'd watched on the lawn. He was fighting for his life and bravely doing what he could.

"I watched the pigs tear Jancek apart." I shuddered. "It was horrible. There wasn't even enough of him..."

Jean-Louis nodded. "I know. Not only do the pigs kill, but they eat their prey. They're omnivores. We've had several people go missing with no trace."

"But now the Huszars know about the tunnel! They're bound to come after you, us, attack us with no notice!" If I hadn't taken a pain pill, I'd have been hyperventilating by now. Hysteria was just a breath away.

"They don't know about the tunnel. We were seen by an owl. Jancek was attacked by the feral pigs. Those are just animals. They can't tell the Huszars what they saw or why they attacked. If we'd been caught by a shapeshifter things would have been different, but by the time they got there, all they saw was a demon, probably on a recon mission, trying to get away from the pigs. The Weres just left it alone."

"So you weren't hurt?"

"Only my ego!" Jean-Louis' tone was light but his face was outlined with worry. "I let one of our best demons, one very close to me, get hurt tonight and another one get torn to pieces. I'm not happy."

Chapter Twenty-four

Even with the pain pill, every time I closed my eyes I saw Jancek being ripped apart and heard the victory squeals of the pigs. It wasn't a restful sleep.

Elise brought coffee and told me it was after 3 in the afternoon. Jazz had called twice and Taras was impatiently waiting for a call back. I threw my legs over the edge of the bed and was reminded about last night when my ankle throbbed in protest.

"Oh, crap, what am I going to do with this?" I pointed at my swollen foot.

"You're to stay off it as much as you can. And I found a walking cane. And see what else I found." Elise pointed to a pair of soft cotton drawstring pants that I'd used in a short-lived foray into yoga. "These will fit loosely enough. If you want to take a shower, I'll rewrap your ankle when you're done."

In minutes, I was clean, wrapped, coffee-ed and behind my desk, with my foot up on a stool, my Bluetooth in my ear, Skype on my monitor and strings of email waiting to be answered. I tackled Jazz first.

"Well, we've sure stirred up a wasp's nest." Her voice was cheery, even though it was after midnight. "It's not slopping over to the magazine yet, but the broadcast guys are running around squawking. "

"What's gotten to them?"

"It's the first show out of Kiev. The clip on the party with the Azerbaijani people? There's a rumor going around that the U.S. State Department wants to talk to us."

"The *STATE* Department! Oh, lord, give me peace. What right do they have to tell us what we can and can't cover."

"I don't know exactly what they want to talk to us about, but I've given them the line. 'I'll tell Ms. Gwenoch to get in touch with you as soon as possible.' I'm sure they've already gone over your head and talked to the Baron."

I sighed. "Yeah, they probably have. Luckily, he's still asleep so I have some time to talk to Taras and a couple of other people before I talk to him. What else?"

"Mira sent some absolutely sin-sexy pictures from the Rio beaches, warming up to summer. I've OK'd a lot of them, but I emailed you and Jean-Louis some that I think need photoshopping. The girls are beautiful, but we've got quite a bit of nipple. Probably all right for the Portuguese edition, and some of the European editions, but I'm not sure they'll go in the States. And those are the ones where they're wearing bikinis!"

Her down-to-earth bubbly laugh came through the earbud and brightened my afternoon. God, there were times when I missed this young woman, with her mixture of hipness and naïveté. I fought a sudden rush of homesickness.

"Speaking of J-L, how are things in *that* department?"

"Things are fine. He's, well we've all, been busy with the Kiev expansion. Boy, we thought handling U.S. notables was nervy! The oligarchs are something else. They're all nouveau-riche and this torrent of money has undone them. They want to flaunt it, so they spend on women, houses, jewels, art, yachts...you name it. And they want people to know about it, but they want to control the amount of information that goes out.

"We're spending more time than we want to on salving egos and calming ruffled feathers."

This was the truth, but Jazz didn't need to know that a chunk of this calming and salving was for the Huszars.

She chuckled again. "They probably never heard of a free press!"

I laughed too, but this cut close to the bone. We operated as a U.S, media corporation, but in fact, the holding company was a closed family corporation registered in

Liechtenstein and I didn't know what their First Amendment, Hah!, regulations were.

I thanked her for the book, didn't tell her what happened when I was reading it, and hung up.

Well, the U.S. State Department. Taras was definitely next on my call list.

He'd gotten a call from the Ukraine First Ministry who'd been contacted by the Azerbaijan Ambassador who'd had a call from the Azerbaijani President. The message was the same. How did you get those videos? Don't use them again. Don't shoot any more pictures.

The "or else" was implied.

He was a tad nervous, but he'd been doing business in this part of the world for many years.

"Do you think the threats are serious?"

I watched him tap a pencil as he thought. "Serious? Well, they're pretty upset, but so far all the messages have been in diplomatic terms. Nothing overt, like 'I know where your children go to school'. Of course, they do know, and they know that I know they know, so it doesn't have to be said."

"Do we need to do anything for you?" I needed to back Taras with all that I had during this edgy time.

"No, my visibility and SNAP's visibility in the world are enough to keep this level threat away. We have plenty of other stuff, we don't have to mess with the them."

"How are you set for the next few days?"

"We've been getting feeds from the Baltic area and the Poles are tickled to have our coverage. They have a growing fashion culture and want to get better ties to the West so are always sending us tips and clips. And the first two issues of SNAP: The Magazine are pretty much laid out."

We had a winner in Taras. Capable, professional; experienced in his region. The only worries I had in Kiev now were the holdovers from Leonid.

"Well, I understand from my U.S. assistant that the State Department wants to chat with us, so I'll probably get an earful when I see the Baron. I'll let you know if we need to go any further. Thanks so much for everything."

The Baron. The State Department. I couldn't take this on while wearing yoga pants. I hobbled over to the closet dressing area and, with Elise's help, chose a long, loose gown that would cover most of the swelling, but wasn't so long I'd trip if I had to walk. Shoes were one shoe of a pair of Gucci flats.

When Jean-Louis knocked on my door, he was surprised to see me up and ready.

"Do you think you should be on that foot?" He looked rested and a low glimmer was back. Well, of course he'd had more than eight hours of uninterrupted sleep and I'd had eight hours of being chased by feral pigs.

I stood up and he laughed. "No, you shouldn't be up on that foot. Why did I ask? You never listen to me, but I don't remember you being so short!"

"Hey Buster, where do you get off calling me short!" I stood as tall as my five-foot-eight allowed. "You know how tall I am."

"I do, but I'm used to seeing you dressed for dinner wearing heels. Those flats take you down a notch."

I glared at him, turned to get the walking cane and found myself in his arms, not being held, being carried.

"I don't think you'll need that," he nodded at the cane, "but I'll have a demon bring it down anyway. The doctor told you to keep off that foot and the demons are ready to carry you wherever you need to go. But for tonight, this pleasure is mine." His head came down to mine. I wrapped my arms around his neck and met his mouth in a long kiss that made me go limp in his arms.

Chapter Twenty-five

Dinner was the four of us plus two men I didn't know.

Jean-Louis settled me in a chair, pulled over an ottoman and introduced them as two of SNAP's attorneys from London.

From London? What was up?

Thank God, tonight's conversation was in English. I didn't miss any of the ins and outs while they discussed the U.S. State Department.

This seemed ludicrous. Why would the State Department be the least bit interested in a gossip show's clip from some tiny country that wasn't even a country until twenty or so years ago?

The word was oil.

Azerbaijan had oil resources and sat in the middle of a web of pipelines and refineries that provided oil to U.S. allies across Eastern Europe.

The State Department didn't want any upset in the fabric of treaties and agreements that kept oil flowing and allies true.

"We don't want to take a stance that will raise hackles, but we need to have entities understand that there is freedom to pursue what we see as a legitimate story." The Baron turned to one of the attorneys, a button-down Englishman who, I suspected, had given his rolled umbrella to Josef as he came in.

"Yes, Baron, that is a fine line we need to walk. And it's more complicated by the nature of your company. The United States doesn't have any direct authority over you, but you want to be sure you respond as a concerned business. I don't think there's any trace of libel here. The people in the clip are public figures and the party was an official function. I think just a note of apology to State and one to the Azerbaijanis should be enough." The solicitor took a bite of roast beef, a proper British meal the staff had put together.

"What if we want to pursue a story about that part of the world?" I don't like people telling me to back off.

"We might want to contact another U.S. media company. One that's more attuned to finding and reporting on touchy stories." Jean-Louis glanced at me with a look that said "Stop right there!"

True, we weren't a media company that dug for hard stories. We didn't have a staff of hundreds of investigative reporters. We had employees who looked good in front of the camera, who could write a thirty second story about a celebrity and pull the appropriate clip, who could spot fashion and entertainment trends, who knew which paparazzi could be relied on.

Looking for links between U.S. allies and trading partners was miles from our comfort zone and I acknowledged this with a small nod to Jean-Louis.

The attorneys were going back to London on one of the Baron's planes, so we said good-byes, good-nights and ta-tas.

Then we started talking.

Was this going to make any difference in our coverage? Was this going to affect our Kiev bureau? Was this going to add fuel to the Huszars fire? Did this have any influence on their new cottage industry of contract killings?

"I think a note of apology to the Azerbaijanis and another one the State Department is in order." The Baron took Pen's hand, a gesture of intimacy that I seldom saw between them. I guessed if you'd been together as a couple for more than 400 years, you knew what your partner felt and constant contact wasn't necessary, still it gave me a warm spot.

"I agree. Our actions and goals in that part of the world don't need a lot of scrutiny." Jean-Louis was absently staring at the Baron and Pen's linked hands. "We need to keep our skirts clean if we plan to bring the Huszars into the fold."

Keep our skirts clean? Into the fold? Had Jean-Louis turned English on me? I gave him an odd look.

"What?"

"I just wondered where those English expressions came from."

"Simply because I talk to you in what you Americans insist is the English language, doesn't mean that I can't also speak English when I want."

I was so startled that my eyes got round. I just stared at him.

"Sorry, my love, I didn't mean to get all shirty—another English expression—with you. I guess the stress of the past two days is showing."

He turned to the Baron. "On a related note, I spoke with Nikoly today. He's planning to go home tomorrow."

"Good, good. Silver poisoning is dangerous. I'm glad we could give him the quiet he needed to recuperate. He's much too valuable to lose. I suspect if he hadn't been ill, we could have made a better accommodation about this silly Azerbaijani issue." The Baron put Pen's hand in her lap and picked up a glass of Bull's Blood.

"Is there anything we need to do to follow up on last night's problem?"

Problem? The Baron called watching a demon being torn apart a problem?

"No. I've heard from Karoly. Actually, the attack helped pull any suspicion away from him and Bohdan because they just joined the frenzy when the shapeshifters realized who the pigs' quarry was. They got kudos from Matthais for being so quick to respond.

"As an aside, the regulars in the village were happy to get the pig carcasses. Wild boar is a treat, but they don't hunt them much any more. One doesn't wonder why."

We adjourned to the media room, watched two editions of SNAP, commented on changes that needed to be made and chatted about the new talent that Mira had found on the beaches of Rio.

Because they operated at such a high level, and kept so many balls in the air, I tended to forget that these three vampires had been the driving force that created an enormous multi-national company .with influence across the globe. This was now, but they were then, putting together the pieces, designing the company, training other family members, hiring staff, learning enough of the technical end that they could oversee it, choosing the celebrities to cover.

As one of the first true celebs, Pen had a long run as a SNAP headliner. I was idly looking at her, wondering if she missed all the adulation and limelight. She shook her head. "That was only one part of my life, my dear." She smiled. "I have so much, much more. Perhaps some day I'll share it with you."

Damn these vampires! I wasn't sure I'd ever learn to shield my thought from them.

Jean-Louis looked at me and smiled, with an invitation in his eyes. "I don't want you to shield your thoughts from me. Perhaps it's time I carried you to your rooms."

Chapter Twenty-six

Once upstairs, I didn't shield much from Jean-Louis.

I'd certainly had my shares of affairs, short-time attractions and even a couple of long-term lovers, but I'd never known a man so attuned to my wants as he was. He was the epitome of the Pointer Sisters' "Slow Hands" and that played in my head for the next hour or so while we made languorous love..

And that night he stayed with me, letting me fall asleep with my arms around him and my head on his chest. Of course he'd had to go to his apartment and sleep through the day, but my body still throbbed from his touch.

The realies hit when I woke the next afternoon. Elise was standing beside me. "Maxie, Maxie." Her voice was soft but insistent and dragged me back from that deep well of pleasure to, "Francois is on the phone. He is adamant."

"Francois? Why is he awake? All right, all right, I'm up. Can you please get me some coffee?"

Elise usually was eager to please, but today she gave me a waspish look and nodded at the steaming cup on my desk.

Oops. I threw on a sleep-shirt and grabbed the phone. "Francois? What's so urgent that got both of us out of bed early?"

"Maxie, we need to go to Poland."

"That got you up in the daylight? Poland? And what's this 'we' business?"

I could hear him chewing his nails across the communication satellites.

"Things are exploding there. We need, you and I, to get there soonest and smooth it out."

"OK, I can be there tomorrow..."

"No, no, we must get there tonight! The Ludvoc designers have pulled all our press credentials for the showings tomorrow! We have them slotted in as the anchor for the French edition tomorrow night and the centerpiece of this week's magazine!"

"Oh, for God's sake! What happened?"

"I don't know. My office got a call a couple of hours ago about it. They debated waking me, but finally knew they had to. I've called three times, and Elise kept saying 'She's sleeping'! What's going on? Are you on vampire time?"

"No, I fell and twisted my ankle, so took a pain pill." He didn't need to know what else kept me up late last night, that was way TMI.

"I'm almost ready. A car is picking me up and one of the planes is waiting at Orly. I'll meet you at the private terminal in Krakow with a car."

"I can be ready to go in less that half-an-hour. Where are we staying? How long do you expect we'll have to be there?"

"We're staying in Krakow and I'd think two days at the outside. If we can't get it fixed early tomorrow, we've got to drop back to something else. I already have the staff here pulling prepared stories and searching clips, just in case."

"Krakow? Ludvoc Designs is in Warsaw."

"Yep, but they thought that having their new spring collection shown against the places in the older city would stress Poland's long history while they're also a current leader in the fashion world."

There weren't many loopy ideas that fashion designers would throw out. Anything to get themselves known, and get them a leg up, in the high-fashion, high-dollar world of international dressing. Well, not strictly dressing. This world was far above the one populated by people who put clothes on to keep warm.

"Fine, I'll get Sandor to make the arrangements and I'll see you later this evening. By the way, I'm still limping a little, so running isn't part of the game. Maybe the Poles will take pity on me. I'll bring my cane."

Elise doesn't really eavesdrop, but hears enough that she anticipates. By the time I'd hung up and was limping my way to the bathroom, she laid out a cashmere dress with a slightly flared skirt and a matching jacket for traveling and was packing a bag.

"I think two business suits and one long dress should do it." I was stripping for a shower.

"Yes. I'll pack the black Chanel gown. I think the Poles need to see elegance." She was busy folding and choosing lingerie when we both stopped and said "Shoes!"

I smiled, she grinned, and put in one more pair of black satin flats. My Gucci's would have to do for business wear.

"Stick in a pair of sneakers, too. I may be able to get them on tomorrow to a take a quick walk. Sitting around will make me cranky."

Within 30 minutes, Sandor picked me up and carried me to the waiting limo.

"All is ready. Hermann is with you here." He indicated another large man all in black, in the passenger's seat. "Ludwig is waiting at the plane. They will both accompany you."

He gave me a pleading look, as much as a demon could. "Please do not go away from them. Jean-Louis will be very angry."

Since Jean-Louis wasn't even up yet, I realized that this plea was from Sandor, himself. Was he concerned for my skin or just for his? I gave him the benefit of the doubt and agreed that I'd stick with the demons. He was probably watching out for both of us.

The demon Hermann was at the plane and he and Ludwig got me and the small amount of luggage settled, took their seats at the back of the cabin and we were up. It was a short flight, the demons reversed their loading routine, and all of us—Francois, me, Hermann, Ludwig—were in another SNAP Mercedes, heading into the ancient city of Krakow.

I had to hand it to Ludvoc Designs for choosing Krakow as a backdrop for their fashions. Since I'd started hanging around with the Kandeskys, I'd developed a very different sense of time. Back home, things that happened before the Revolutionary War, like the founding of Monterey, were precious few and venerated. Here in Europe, 1775 was practically yesterday so Krakow, founded in 1000, was old but not ancient.

But it was beautifully preserved because the last time it was sacked was in the 13th century by the Tartars. It hadn't suffered much in WWII as Poland was invaded and fell in September 1939. In fact, it was one of Europe's best-preserved medieval cities, was named a World Heritage Site in the 1970s and was a European City of Culture in 2000.

We had a fast tour of the medieval city center, where the shows would be held beginning the next day, and then bundled into a spacious penthouse that SNAP had reserved.

It was far easier to rent or lease apartments when it was the regular SNAP employees, like me. We just needed a basic hotel space. But traveling with demons and vampires entailed a lot more. Demons didn't need much in the way of accommodations beyond a secure, locked room for their weapons (a locking bathroom was usually fine) plus a couple of beds.

They always did their own security sweep, slightly more rigorous now that Chechens were in the picture.

But the Kandeskys needed a dedicated place in an interior room with no exterior light. They didn't travel with coffins, but did have their own pillows and of course their own food. I'd never asked (I thought it was rude) but assumed that the pillows were partially filled with Hungarian soil. And baggage always included at least a case of Bull's Blood and a couple of ice chests.

Once all was settled, Francois and Hermann left to plot out the best spots for our paparazzi, assuming that we could get our press passes back. I was meeting with the

Ludvoc Design group to beg, wheedle, threaten, to find out what happened. That had to start early, because the first runway was scheduled to kick off at dusk, 5:30 p.m., against the lights of the 13th century Main Market Square and the 16th century facade of the Cloth Hall, two of the most imposing medieval buildings.

And that left Francois a slim slice of time to get all the photographers situated.

He and Hermann came back before midnight and we had a fast Skype conversation with Jean-Louis, filling him in on the plans and sharing a sketch Francois had done of the main runway sites.

"Have you found out why the passes were pulled?" Jean-Louis' face was grim, his voice all business.

"No." Francois was glum. "Maxie's going to meet with the Ludvoc group first thing in the morning."

"Who are you taking with you?" Jean-Louis was asking me...what? Who were my babysitters? Who would negotiate with the Ludvoc designers? He could see my face screwing up to make a snarky remark.

"Poland isn't too far afield for the Chechens. You must have at least two demons with you."

"Maxie," Francois broke in. "Jean-Louis is right. Plus, this is still an area that respects a strong man and having two bodyguards means you have protection. It's a sign of your strength and, more importantly, SNAP's strength, to show up with an entourage."

"Thank you, Francois. We'll appeal to her vanity!"

I came close to losing it at that crack.

"I'm not vain, I just want to do things for myself." I slapped my hand down on the table we were using as a desk, then curbed my rising anger. They were right, we needed to go in with a solid show of strength, otherwise the news that a small Polish fashion house had faced down the mighty Kandeskys and SNAP would be around the circuit faster than the discount knock-off designs.

"I'm taking Hermann and Ludwig; they both know the city and the Poles."

"Thank you." Some of the tension went out of Jean-Louis' face. "Please let me know as soon as you find anything out. And take care of yourself, you know I worry."

Chapter Twenty-seven

The Ludvoc Design group had taken over a Baroque building around the corner from the Main Market for the duration of the three-day show and it was barely controlled chaos that morning. Hair and make-up people swarmed, models stood around in their underwear smoking, photographers shouted at assistants for better light, aides trundled long racks of clothes and one poor guy kept yelling for shoes.

I led my little parade of demons, one carrying my cane and one carrying my briefcase, to the offices at the back. I'd unwrapped my ankle and was wearing my Gucci flats, so I acted as though our entrance was just business as usual and the designers' staff took us at our word. I was ushered into a small office and given a chair. The demons stood behind me. We looked formidable.

The head of the Ludvoc Design Group, Victor, reached over to shake my hand and ordered coffee for us. "I am happy to meet you Ms. Gwenoch. I have long been an admirer of SNAP."

My right eyebrow arched. "Hummmm, that's interesting, Victor. I've been told that our press passes for your Spring Show have been cancelled. Would you care to tell me about that?"

He didn't expect my directness. Business wasn't usually done so bluntly, and seldom by a woman, so Victor was slightly out of his element. He turned as a minion brought in coffee and fussed a bit about getting it served, an interruption that gave him a few minutes to compose himself and find excuses.

"It's true, we did cancel your press passes, but that's

because we were told you would be part of pool coverage this year."

Good save. SNAP was *never* part of pool coverage, and I suspected Victor knew this. Pool coverage was when a group of end-users, tabloids, smaller magazines and newspapers together hired a photographer and then shared the images. This was not something that SNAP ever did. If the event was small, we would buy from freelancers, but if we ever found that the freelancer had sold to another outlet as well, he or she was banned from SNAP forever. Not a price that most freelancers were willing to pay.

"Who told you that we were part of a pool this year?" I picked up my coffee and sipped, surprised that it was so good.

"We got an email and a phone call. I can show you the email." He picked up a cell and gave a paragraph or so of order in Polish. Within a minute, another staffer came in with a piece of paper, what looked like a copy of an email.

Victor was right in one regard. The email was headed with the SNAP logo and sent from the L.A. office. Or what looked like the L.A. office. Looked at carefully, it was clear that our account had been hacked.

"Didn't you wonder about this? Didn't you follow up?"

"We did. We called the number in the email and were told that it was correct. That someone in your French office had approved it."

"Well, this is all fake. No one approved pool coverage. And the head of our Paris office is here right now, working with our photographers to finalize shooting sites."

Victor almost swallowed his tongue with his coffee. "Oh, you can't do that! I've, I mean, we've put out notices that SNAP won't be shooting. Oh, they'll ruin us!"

"Who's 'they'?"

"I don't know who they are. They're the ones who sent us the email and made the phone call!"

I just sat there, staring at him. Not only was it clear he was lying, he was beginning to figure out that we knew he was lying. Finally, one of the demons, Hermann, I think, leaned over and handed me my briefcase. I opened it, pulled out a sheaf of papers and began leafing through them.

Visibly shaken, Victor began stammering in earnest. "They told us you wouldn't find out. They said you'd just assume there was miscommunication between your offices. They said that they'd make sure you got copies of the pool pictures."

"And again, who is this 'they'?"

"I really don't know. I mean, I'm not sure. The phone call did come from Paris, caller ID showed the right city code. I never got a call from SNAP before, so how was I to know it wasn't from you?"

"Did you ask for any verification?"

"No! They, the man, said he was calling for Maxie Gwenoch. I didn't question. And then..." his voice trailed off.

"And, then...?"

"I got another call. This time the voice had an accent, not a French accent, an Eastern accent, maybe Slavic."

"And the voice said?"

Victor shook his head, his skin gray. Clearly this was a conversation he didn't want to remember.

"The voice said if I wanted our design studio to continue, we had to do what they said. We had to cancel your press passes and make sure you were only given pool pictures. You, SNAP, weren't to be allowed to cover the show in any way. No runway seats, no backstage passes, no model or designer interviews. And by keeping you away from the runway, you wouldn't even be able to know who was there and who ordered."

This was interesting. Not only were the fashion pictures taken away, a big pain, but we'd have no idea who was there. Our vaunted celeb coverage would be out the window.

And this could be from a wide range of interests. What leapt to mind first was the Huszars trying to move in on our cash cows, part of the skeleton of our success. Next, were the oligarchs, who wanted their privacy kept private. Then, and this was scary to think about, a pact between them. Or even the Chechens, thinking they could sell their muscle to either or both groups, and doing it on spec. They didn't need to have a contract, they could peddle the results to the highest bidder.

We seemed to have stirred up every baddie in Europe and they all wanted a piece of us. The price of success!

I watched Victor. He was quivering. "What are you going to do?"

"I think the question is 'What are YOU going to do?' We're going to cover your Spring Show."

Victor closed his eyes. I thought he was going to vomit. He managed to take a few deep breaths.

"We're done, then. I just wanted to start a fashion house. Do some great designs, carve out a place for us in the new Eastern economy. I thought this would help Poland gain stature and respect in the West." I could almost hear him moan.

"What are you talking about? Why do you think you're done?"

"They'll kill us. Or they'll take us over. They'll send in thugs to make sure our orders never get shipped. They'll scare off our suppliers..."

Victor was listing a tale of mayhem that made even me nervous. "We're going to be your partner. SNAP will provide some guards," I waved my hand toward the demons, "to watch your shipments, if need be. We'll put the word out that, in the interests of U.S. and European harmony, we're going to bat for struggling businesses in the former Eastern Bloc. You can say that you have a contract for SNAP to cover your shows for the next three years.

"That alone will ensure that all the fashion and gossip outlets will cover you and should make your shows sell-outs. If the fashionistas think they'll be on the pages of SNAP, they'll turn out."

I couldn't have made Victor any happier if he'd been on the Titanic and I'd thrown him the last life preserver.

"Do you mean that? Will SNAP really do that?" Sweat was beading his forehead. "Why would you do that after I pulled your press passes?"

"Because you acted in what you thought was the best way to protect your business. You were threatened by very bad forces and you didn't see any way out but to obey them. This was not of your doing."

"Thank you, Ms. Gwenoch. I couldn't see beyond the threats and didn't know what else to do."

I stood up, more to stretch out my ankle then to walk out. "The next time you get what looks like an email or fax or letter or phone call from SNAP, you call either Francois or me. I will send you our cell phone numbers on a secure line. Do not EVER give those numbers out. And only use them to verify that we've been in touch with you. Keep all conversations to less than a minute."

"Will you attend our party after the show tonight?"

"Yes, Francois and I will be there. I hope everything goes well."

Hermann, Ludwig and I walked out of the office and back into pandemonium, which seemed to have increased in volume and tone.

Once back in the limo, I asked them to give me a better tour of the city, so for a couple of hours we crossed and re-crossed the Vistula River while watching tourists, locals and some of the more than 100,000 students who attended the universities of this city.

We did not go to Auschwitz . The Poles hadn't built that death pit and it wasn't a part of their history I wanted to see.

Chapter Twenty-eight

"**W**ell done, Maxie!" Jean-Louis' voice was buoyant. "That should send a strong message we're not backing down. Are you all right?"

I was all right. I was more than all right. For the first time in months I felt powerful and that I was actively guiding my actions. Until now, I hadn't acknowledged that being a victim, or being seen as one at least, had sapped me. I hadn't fought back, except with Jean-Louis, and that was such a mixture of personal and professional concern that I felt paralyzed much of the time.

"I'm fine. And even my ankle's fine. It really gave Victor heart to hear that we considered him a partner. When I saw the 'email' from SNAP I knew we'd been hacked. It looked like our logo and had our L.A. address. I suppose if you'd never done business with us, you might not know we never use pool coverage. I couldn't totally fault Ludvoc designs."

"Who do you think sent it?"

Wow, Jean-Louis was asking my advice? Naw, he was just checking to see if my assumptions were the same as his.

"I'm not sure. The list of folks we've riled up is the size of the Krakow phone book. Could be the Huszars, wanting to discredit us. Could be the Chechens, wanting themselves to look good. Could be some combination."

"That's where I'm going, too, although I'm detecting the hand of the Huszars, Matthais, ultimately behind this. Are you going to the runway show?"

"I am. Victor has reserved front row seats for us. I'm taking Hermann and Francois will meet us later at the party.

That'll put the wind up Matthais' nose, to see our coverage and me right in his face!"

We shared a laugh, but his voice got wary. "Please don't take any chances. And keep Hermann and Ludwig close. Know that I love you."

All of my work trying to explain how I felt when he "took care of" me hadn't fallen on deaf ears. We were now partners in this deathly war.

I pulled myself together with a Chanel business suit for the runway show. I'd come back later, change into the gown and pick up Francois for the party. Hermann and I headed out. I didn't think I needed both demons. This was a big event, all invited guests, Ludvoc Designs would have their own security and we'd be deep in the crowd in the first row off the runway.

The design studio did itself proud. The dresses and casual clothes for spring were floaty, gauzy pastels, very romantic. Prints looked like Impressionist watercolors, soft-lined and indistinct, just waiting for an invitation for a picnic on the river. Of course, any woman who'd wear one of these creations for a picnic was either crazy or incredibly wealthy. The simple dresses would be running close to $5,000 at the studio.

If the mass market followed Ludvoc Designs though, knockoff versions would be available at big department stores for around $150 right after Christmas.

We were just standing up after the last of the bows and applause when a commotion broke out where guests were streaming out the exit. I couldn't see with all the people crowding around, plus Hermann was keeping himself between me and anything interesting, and the shouts were in yet another language I didn't know—probably Polish.

Hermann swiveled his head around, almost yelling Hungarian into his communicator, while looking for another exit. He spotted a path around the runway and through the backstage into the dressing area, grabbed me around the waist and half-carried me out of the audience. Once in the dressing area, Victor rushed over.

"Please don't be alarmed. This was just a student protest. There are many students, Poles and others, who think what we do is frivolous and not worthy of interest. There are so many other issues we're facing. The economy, membership in the European Union, the loss of our heritage, and loss of the zloty."

I knew there was an undercurrent of angst in many of the EU countries over the euro becoming the currency and Britain refusing to give up the pound. These were old and proud nations who'd fought bitterly with one another for centuries and now were yoked together, so flashes of discontent were bound to erupt now and again.

"Thank you. I am a little on edge. I'm going to the hotel to change and meet Francois, who's going over some images that we'll use tonight. We'll be back for the party."

Hermann moved the crowd aside and as we headed back to the limo the security forces had pushed back a group of young people holding placards and shouting some slogan. I raised my eyebrows and in rusty English, Hermann said, "My Polish is not so good, but I think they say 'Keep zloty'."

How wonderful to find a ruckus that had nothing to do with the Huszars!

At the hotel, I managed to get myself into the long Chanel gown, put my hair up and redo my makeup without Elise, but I didn't like it. I was getting way used to the luxe life.

The party was a rush of noise, sweaty bodies, happiness, Champagne and over-amped club music. Hermann and Ludwig stuck to me like glue, leaving Francois to manage on his own. I felt too old for this young, hip group and I flagged down Francois to tell him I was leaving.

"OK, Maxie. I'm going to stay and see what I can find." His eyes roved the crowded dance floor and his shoulders arm-danced. "See you later," and he slithered toward the bar.

Once outside in the clear, cold air, I remembered again that smoking was still a staple in this part of the world. Suddenly, Hermann opened the limo door, shoved me into the back, hopped in after me and rattled off instructions into his communicator. The demon driving knew Krakow, because he took off and floored it while maneuvering through the narrow, twisty streets of the old town.

Both Hermann and Ludwig were talking top speed into communicators while checking their Sig Sauers for ammo magazines. I twisted around and saw headlights behind us, getting closer, but couldn't tell what kind of vehicle it was.

"Who is it?" It was useless for me to ask. English wasn't a viable language for these demons, so hanging on and hoping was the best alternative I had. The chase only lasted a few minutes. The driver headed for a gated door into an underground garage and, at the last second, the door rolled up, we were through and the door slammed down again.

We circled down a floor, parked next to an elevator, Hermann practically shoved me out and into the elevator and punched a button. That's when I realized we were in the hotel, in an elevator that only went to the penthouse suite. And me, thinking we'd checked into a hotel just like normal people. Life with the vampires was never dull.

Once in the suite, the demons called Sandor to report in. That, of course, alerted Jean-Louis, who called my cell, frantic.

"What happened? The last report I got was only a student protest over zlotys! Who was it?"

I couldn't tell him because I didn't know. "I only saw headlights through the rear window. Hermann and Ludwig were on their communicators, but they weren't speaking English, or even Hungarian. I don't know the demon who was driving, but he knew what he was doing."

"I'm getting reports from Sandor. Some of the demons stationed in Poland are tracking the car now. I'll call you again when I have more information. By the way, where's Francois?"

Francois? I hadn't a clue. "I'm not sure. I'll find him and get back to you."

Beyond calling Francois' cell, I didn't even know how to

look for him. I got his voicemail. I called Victor also, with the excuse of checking with Francois on some of the images. He hadn't seen Francois. I could have used a little vampire mind-reading right about now.

Finally, Hermann got off the call to Sandor and I asked him how I could find Francois. "He is with other demons, chasing the car. They will call when catched."

Well, with a vampire and a few demons after them, whoever was following us was probably sorry now.

Chapter Twenty-nine

Francois showed up about 3 a.m.

"Well, Maxie, an interesting night," was what he said by way of greeting.

"So, interesting can cover a multitude of sins, and a lot of meanings. What the hell happened? When I left, you were trolling the bar for a hot one."

He gave a quick grin and nodded. "I was. And I'd found one. Not a donor, well not yet, but possibilities. And then my cell rang and that was the end of that. Hermann had called in support, a car was waiting and we were less than five minutes behind you."

Damn the vampire, he was cagey enough that I still didn't know whether his intended prey was male or female.

"So who was it?"

"Who was what? Oh, you mean following you? It was a low-ranking Huszar with two Chechens. We caught up with them when they slowed to try and figure out how to breach the security gate. Took 'em off to a little place down by the river. Had a little chat." Francois was relishing the 1930s movie gangster-speak.

"Are they dead?"

"The two Chechens are. I thought that was a good message to go back to their pals. Sure, the Huszars may pay well, but the thugs are losing soldiers, too. We sent the Huszar back with a serious case of silver poisoning. A little pay-back for Nikoly."

That was our answer then. Huszars and Chechens hacked our computers and sent fake emails out. And they were working together. It was time to discuss this with Jean-Louis.

We called him, gave him the bare bones. He'd get the IT guys going on tracing the email path, close down the hacked sites and set up new ones. He'd call another meeting with Karoly and some of his followers, he'd get Chaz and Carola in L.A. started on a disinformation campaign and we'd have a giant strategy meeting tomorrow night at the castle.

With that, I went to bed. For Francois, it was mid-afternoon, but I'd been up since 7 a.m., first getting ready for the meeting with Victor, then the tour of Krakow, the runway show, the party and the chase scene. I was wiped.

I ordered the plane for 10 a.m., figuring that I'd get back to the castle in time for a nap before the big meeting, but got hit with a ton of calls and emails. Jazz was concerned because L.A. was planning to use images from the Krakow show, but was still under the impression that they may have been shot by a pool photographer. And while I had her on Skype, Chaz joined the conversation, which meant that I had to go over the talk with Victor, and the resolution, with both of them.

"And Chaz, we need to draw up some sort of contract language that we'll cover Ludvoc Designs' show for the next three years. But keep any language out of it about using the images. If what I saw last night is any indication, they're a talented group and will do well. If for some reason they don't hit the big time, we don't want to get stuck running pictures of nobodies at sparsely attended shows in Poland. Promoting good will with our allies isn't the purpose of SNAP."

Then there was time spent with Taras. He, too, had heard about the chase and wanted to find out if any of the Chechens were from Kiev. I couldn't answer that and turned him over to Sandor, who may have been able to track down the dead. Taras' fear was that if the dead guys were part of the Ukraine branch, they may set up retaliation and he could get caught in a cross-fire that wasn't of his making.

After he talked with Sandor, he called back to say that they'd tracked the dead Chechens to Georgia. "I can bet the head guys aren't happy with dead soldiers, but at least we're not the shooters in Ukraine. Things are heating up, so please take care of yourself."

Great, was someone I hardly knew treating me like a victim now? Then I did a mental head-slap. That was just a polite thing to say. Now that I was feeling in control again, I didn't need to sabotage myself with fears and doubts.

Then there was a call to Francois. He wasn't back in the office yet, but they expected him late that night. So I called his cell and left a voicemail.

By this time, I only had an hour to get ready for dinner and the meeting. It was enough time that I let Elise pamper me by running a bath instead of a quick shower, but it left me so relaxed I asked her to make me an espresso as well.

I went for dressy business, with a silk suit, but stuck with flats again. Just as I was finishing my make-up, Francois called. "Allo, Maxie, are you rested after our fun last night?"

"Fun? I'm not sure I'd call it that. Are you on your way back to the office?"

"*Mais, non.* I'm staying in Krakow another night."

"Why? Is the photographer still shooting?"

"No, we got plenty last night and some today at a lunch show they put on. I have some unfinished business."

"Oh, Francois, you're not going after the Chechens again! Taras said they're pissed."

"No, this is my own unfinished business. You remember I saw someone at the bar?"

The lights went on, but how could I find out if it was a man for a woman?

None of my business, I finally decided.

"Have a good time, then! I hope I'll see you soon," and I signed off with a big air kiss as Jean-Louis came in.

"That better have been one of us," he smiled.

God, it was good to see him! I moved from behind the desk to the living room where Elise had put my coffee, but had to sit down again. Just seeing him made my legs weak.

"Yep, that was Francois. He's staying in Krakow

another night. He's found somebody he wants to pursue."

Jean-Louis threw back his head and laughed. The good humor and safety of the castle brought back his glimmer and now his aura shimmered around him. "That boy, he needs to be careful. Hasn't he seen what happens when he gets mixed up with a regular? I'd think that my example would be enough to scare him off."

"What's that crack supposed to mean? Have I been a drag on you?"

"Hah, I knew that'd get a rise out of you! Now that you're stronger, stand up so I can hold you and welcome you home properly."

Home?

I stood up, feeling short in my flats, and wound my arms around his neck. We'd deal with the "home" issue later. He leaned over me and gave me a kiss that took my breath away as his tongue probed my mouth and he gently sucked my bottom lip between his teeth.

"Stop, stop," I managed to gasp.

He pulled back and looked at me, hurt beginning to grow in his eyes. "You want me to stop?"

"Just for now. If that keeps up, in one minute I'm going to strip my clothes off and ruin my hair and makeup that Elise slaved over." Since he'd pulled back slightly, I was able to take a deep breath. "My love, I can't keep you and business together in my head right now. This is not an area I can multi-task in. It's either you or the Baron, dinner and the meeting. Just being in the same room with you tonight is going to be hard for me."

The hurt faded from his eyes and was replaced with impish humor. "Ah ha, I have you in my power and later tonight I will have my way with you!"

"Is that a promise?"

"Oh, yes, yes it is, love. But for now, dinner and a command performance." He opened the door with a flourish and a demon fell into the room.

"I am so sorry, Jean-Louis." The demon was stammering in his embarrassment. "Sandor ordered me to come and get you. They are waiting dinner."

"Well, tell Sandor that we're on our way," my glorious vampire said as he took my arm.

Chapter Thirty

Dinner passed peacefully enough.

Afterward, we watched the L.A. show that included footage of the Ludvoc's Spring Show. Francois had done a superb job assigning sites for the photographers, and Krakow's medieval Main Market was a spectacular backdrop to the gauzy fashions. He even had a short video clip, a mini-tour of the city, which showed it off and anchored that it was a World Heritage Site in viewer's minds.

By 11 p.m. we were ready for our guests, so Sandor and Jean-Louis headed down the tunnel. They were back shortly with Karoly, Alessandr, Bohdan and another, introduced as Volodymyr Antonovych, who was from Russia but had been turned in Georgia. He wasn't a Chechen, but had spent time in Chechnya so understood the tribal patterns and loyalties.

This was going to be a little tricky with languages, so we had two simultaneous translators, demons who were fluent in many of the Eastern European languages. Jean-Louis would translate into English for me, as I seemed to be the lightning rod for the current unpleasantness.

We started with the kidnap attempt in Kiev. Jean-Louis gave a detailed account, including Nikoly's bout with silver poisoning. I was surprised that he'd willingly let this information out, but he must have felt the Huszars could be trusted.

There was some brief talk about Leonid, who apparently was in the dog house with Matthais for letting us get away. Volodymyr said something in a spate of Russian that turned out to be a discourse on the fact that the Chechens wouldn't let their soldiers die without retribution.

With that piece of cheery news, we segued into the

incident in Krakow. The IT guys had pinged the fake email and the path led right back to a computer at Matthias' castle, surprise, surprise.

"What does Matthais stand to gain with this?" Jean-Louis looked honestly puzzled. "He has to know that tracking an email back to its true point of origin is easy."

"It's not a ruse, it's more of a...a...point of annoyance." Karoly was speaking English for my benefit. "He figures if you get upset, you'll spend time and effort on tracking it, a deflection from his primary plan."

"And that is?" The Baron hadn't said a word but now it seemed he needed to take the lead. "We have so many red herrings that finding our way through is getting tedious."

Karoly sighed and dropped back in Hungarian. With Jean-Louis translating in my ear, the Huszar said, "Ultimately he wants to destroy you, all of you." Karoly looked around the room and registered the Baron, Pen, Jean-Louis, Bela, Milos, me and Sandor, respectfully standing guard at the door. "Not only does he want what you have—the wealth, standing, clout—but all of you personally. Many of us don't understand where his hatred comes from."

"I do," said Jean-Louis, then nodded at the Baron. "We do. And it's not a tale we want to tell now."

It must have been a deep and very dark secret. This was the second time Jean-Louis alluded to it, then refused to go there.

"Beyond that, where is he headed?"

The Huszars exchanged looks. Karoly began. "He had two plans, no, paths, to get to the same end. He's going to throw up as many small incidents as he can, to keep you busy putting out small fires. He's hoping that you'll miss the big one. The big one is him taking over the management and ownership of SNAP."

Jean-Louis choked on his sip of Bulls' Blood. "Take over the management? He doesn't know the first thing about running SNAP!"

"No, but you have how many employees? Twenty-thousand, 30,000 around the world.? And how many of them are regulars? And how many of them can do their jobs regardless of who the CEO is? All he needs to do, he thinks, is take some of your top management, replace it with Huszars who have some training, and SNAP goes on."

He turned to me. "That's why you're so important to his plan. Most of the top management are Kandeskys; you're one of the few regulars. You won't have the strength that the vampires have to resist him. Even if you don't agree to work with him, he can surmount your defenses and go into your mind, your memories, your knowledge. If he can suck your abilities, he, or someone he appoints, can do your job as well as you can."

Now I was scared. I'd gone along thinking that even if one of the Huszars or their goons grabbed me, they still didn't have my background. And naively, I'd thought I could keep it from them. Name, rank and serial number was all I was going to share.

Hah! I didn't even have to open my mouth for them to pull out every atom of my being, throw away what they didn't want and toddle off with the rest. I must have looked stricken. Jean-Louis leaned over and whispered, "That's the business reason I get so concerned about you."

These stakes were much higher than I'd thought. Sure, I was frightened when I'd been grabbed off the beach at Santa Monica. And I thought Jean-Louis overreacted when I'd been shipped off to the castle after that little incident.

Then, Paris. My blood ran cold when I realized what my jaunt to see normal Paris could have cost and why Michele and Denis were so upset when they briefly lost me.

I had to admit, I was frightened by the violence in Kiev. And the aftermath, when I realized that Jean-Louis could be killed was hammered home seeing Nikoly suffering from silver poisoning.

And yes, Jean-Louis had called it war. And I knew there would be violence. Everybody knew that the rise of the oligarchs, the Chechens, the Russian Mafia, brought a new level of viciousness and fear.

I guess I still chose to look at it as a particularly rough-and-tumble business takeover. Certainly more than a proxy fight with buyout threats. But still, a war of commerce that left the participants alive to fight another day.

This, though, was scorched-earth warfare. Participants sucked of all their knowledge and unable to continue. People killed or left for dead. Leadership slain and the company left to live in a climate of fear.

If the Huszars managed to take down the Kandeskys, they would have an international bully pulpit that came into homes every night spewing their message of fear and hatred. The celebs followed by their cameras could be the international terrorists, the world bullies, the corrupt and venal.

They could have control over the information that a huge population around the world got every day. And they could do this without giving up any of their current ways. Simply because the Kandeskys had given up killing to find a more civilized way of feeding, didn't mean that the Huszars must also.

"And they could sell this power, this pulpit, to the highest or strongest bidder." Damn, even Karoly could read my mind! "You begin to see Ms. Maxie, why there are many of us who do not follow Matthais' way. Yes, we like to have power, but we tire of all the violence. Matthais and his Council are always plotting, always sending out spies, always searching for ways to control others. They think that by providing a constant food source they will win the hearts of their followers. What they don't see is that building a following based on fear is dangerous because followers can turn on you."

This was the longest speech I'd ever heard from a Huszar. I thought of them as being vicious and uneducated, but there were some who went beyond that. I'd have to ask Jean-Louis if Karoly approached him or he sought Karoly out.

OK, so Matthais wanted some kind of world

domination, maybe in concert with one of the rogue countries or terrorist leaders. That didn't mean we had to deal with the current threats, the every-day attacks, their ongoing ties to kidnap me.

Jean-Louis turned to Volodymyr and asked for a rundown of the Chechen leaders and tribes. They were speaking Russian, and Jean-Louis was in the midst of the conversation, so I wasn't getting instantaneous translation. One of the demons was trying to keep up in English, and I got the gist if not the nuance.

Volodymyr was describing an almost feudal society, run by the strongest. Who the strongest was, at any given time, could change, so there were shifting or overlapping loyalties. No one trusted anyone else, and a chieftain could have three or four pacts at once, always on the lookout for an alliance with a stronger or richer boss.

I shook my head, a gesture Jean-Louis noticed. "This is difficult. We don't even know who the enemy is, besides the Huszars. How can you fight if you can't see the enemy?"

"Yes, Maxie, you're right, but you forget that we've been dealing with these kinds of shifting sands for centuries. We don't recognize national borders because we've seen them switch so many times. The Ottoman Turks, the Habsburgs, the wars—we've been there. That's one reason we went into business. Money doesn't care who's in charge, it flows to those who can control it. The Chechens, the oligarchs, the Russian Mafia, are transients. The constant is the Huszars and we can't let them divide our energies taking on these recent threats. We have to go after the Hydra's head."

And for the next hour, they devised and debated a plan that left me speechless.

Chapter Thirty-one

I was going to disappear.

Chaz and Carola were preparing a campaign about my disappearance. I was traveling to Frankfurt, being driven. I never arrived. At first SNAP kept it quiet, but when I didn't turn up the next day, they began a search.

Sightings of my limo on the autobahn, leaving the autobahn, at a rest stop just off the autobahn, poured in to SNAP offices all over Germany.

The next day, the police found my limo tucked into a grove of trees behind an autobahn rest stop about 80 km south of Frankfurt.

There were bullet holes in the windows and small spots of blood on the inside of the passenger compartment door. But I was gone, the driver and body guard were gone, my luggage was gone. Just the mute car as a testament that something bad had happened.

It was the lead story on every edition of SNAP, it was the cover of SNAP The Magazine, it was covered on every news cast in the U.S. and most of those in Europe. The police were interviewed and were stumped. The Baron had no comment beyond "We at SNAP are devastated that Ms. Gwenoch has disappeared. And we're mourning the loss of the SNAP employees, as well."

This went on for four days, until some enterprising paparazzi called the Paris office and offered to sell pictures of me and Jean-Louis walking along the Seine just at dusk. It was shot with a long lens and was slightly blurry, but there was no doubt in anyone's mind that it was us.

The jig was up, and we returned to the daily grind,

offering apologies all around and making retribution to the police forces of a couple of countries for all the extra manpower they'd had to bring on for the international search. Media outlets in the U.S. offered editorials and opinions on SNAP pulling such as shoddy trick to gain readers, but they in turn were yelled at for covering the coverage.

All in all, it was one big, fat, cluster-fuck with a lot of people walking away with egg on their faces.

What it had gained us, though, were four precious days with no imminent threats from the Huszars, the Chechens, the Russians or anyone else. And during this time, Jean-Louis put together the most compact, secretive, tightest network of informers—including another hundred or so disaffected Huszars—across Europe and into Asia.

He had trusted people, some vampires, some regulars, in Kiev, Warsaw, Krakow, Sofia, Vienna, Prague, Moscow and Baku. He'd sent a Kandesky demon to head up each branch, equipped everyone with untraceable communications devices and then they sat and waited for the Huszars to make a move.

And because we'd set the scene with a couple of bullet holes in the windshield and a smattering of donor blood, the baddies were in disarray, all wanting to get as far away from this as possible and willing to blame any of the others.

Certainly the Huszars didn't want any of this, they'd spent centuries dodging the blame for anything. Certainly not the Chechens, they had enough trouble with the blowback from their legitimate business ventures and hits. And certainly not the terrorists from a variety of places in the Near East. Kidnapping a gossip journalist was not going to get them gravitas in the eyes of the world community.

The four days weren't all work, though. I had time with him alone and was even allowed to sleep with him during part of the day.

Watching him in action, creating webs, making plans, interacting with other Kandesky family members and demons was like an aphrodisiac for me, not that I needed one where he was concerned.

He was controlled, direct, capable of handling many things at once, and it was clear that all the people he led revered him. And he was mine.

We made love, we talked, we took walks at night and watched Paris light up all her buildings and monuments. And we talked. He talked to me about Magda and told me that her death was when the abiding hatred of the Huszars began.

The families had been rivals for years before he'd met Magda and she hadn't been killed by the Huszars. She'd been killed by a group of villagers who saw her fangs. They didn't care what family she was from, she was a vampire.

And Jean-Louis blamed the Huszars for stirring up that fear because, by then, the Kandeskys had created other ways to feed themselves and no longer attacked the peasants.

He was devastated. The Baron worried about his health. Pen took him to Europe's grand cities and spas, hoping that finding another young, beautiful woman would help his healing. The only thing that helped his healing was time.

"I mourned for almost a hundred years. There was no joy in my life. No beauty. Gradually the fog thinned. I began to be aware of all the beautiful women there were. No one would ever replace Magda, and they were all regulars so I could only spend a little time with each of them but I started to realize that I had an eye for beauty. Many of the women I admired were painted and then as technology advanced, photographed. That's why I'm the art director for SNAP." He laughed. "Well, when I'm not being General, chief strategist, master spy and savior of Maxie."

He ran his hand down the side of my face. I kissed his palm and it continued down my neck and onto the top of my breast. He sucked my earlobe as he gently pinched my nipple then leaned over to take it in his mouth. I was gone.

After being "discovered" in Paris, we had to explain why we'd taken off, so we announced our engagement. We were engaged all right, but it didn't have anything to do with a wedding.

This romantic news though, gave us a bit more time to put some plans into place. There was a flurry of tabloid and gossip coverage of our "engagement" and the Huszars steered clear of us while we were in the limelight. It was one thing when we were *covering* the celebs, it was another when we *were* the celebs.

It was dangerous for the Huszars, the Chechens, other hangers-on, to attack such visible figures, so they laid low and bided their time.

We came home to the castle—I was actually beginning to think of it as "home" but Santa Monica still had a piece of my heart—and fell back into a work routine. I picked up the reins of SNAP again and spent time on the phone and Skype with Jazz.

She was alternately pissed; "Why'd you use me like that? Couldn't you just tell me?" and dying of curiosity, "Have you set a date? Where are you going to be married? Has he given up hitting on other women?"

After that last crack I said, "Enough!" and we got back to business. Part of the reason that Jazz was so upset at us was because she'd gotten calls from other media accusing her of knowing and abetting our "runaway". She'd been tarred with the brush without being part of the action.

She was a trouper, though, and finally said she was glad I was back, was glad I hadn't been hurt and was glad at the "engagement" news.

We were in fine shape for coverage. The large-budget movies were being released for the Christmas season and the run-up to the awards shows, which culminated with the Oscars.

It was late spring, going into summer in South America and Australia so beach shots and sunny get-aways were available and, an answer to our prayers, one of Europe's minor royals was getting married.

The Christmas wedding would have aristos and richies

from across two continents buying dresses, jewelry, hats. We could shoot their shopping sprees, their parties, their travels and then, after all that, the actual wedding. This was good for a minimum of two weeks constant coverage.

After the past couple of weeks of chase-and-be-chased, it felt like a luxury to be back to worrying about the budget for staff to go to a wedding.

Well, at least it wasn't mine.

Chapter Thirty-two

Our little idyll brought calm to the next few days.

Jean-Louis and I worked in my office, companionably reading emails, making notes, holding videoconference meetings, developing the next issues of SNAP.

It was pleasant and peaceful working together. I wondered fleetingly if he and Magda had ever spent time so amiably. He looked over at me. "No, we didn't work together because we didn't have these extensive businesses."

I stuck my tongue out at him.

"I do relish your childishness. You make me feel as though I'm four- or five-hundred years old." He stuck his tongue out at me, which convulsed both of us. God, it was so good to laugh with this man.

"It makes me crazy that you can read me so easily and well."

"I keep telling you that we don't really read minds. It's true, we do have some ability to read your thoughts, but so much of it is just schooling ourselves to read faces, gestures, body language. You could do it, too, if you weren't so impatient and closed off."

"Me? Closed off? There are HUGE parts of you I'll never know. You have centuries of thoughts, events, memories that are in vaults. Every so often I see you open just a crack and a memory or feeling worms its way out."

He humphed and turned back to his laptop screen. *I* was the one closed off? I think not!

I jumped when he said, "See, right there is an example. You swung around in your chair, tossed your head and started pounding on the keys. You didn't have to tell me that you disagreed with me, you showed me."

"Well, I get frustrated with you." Hmmm, this wasn't good, I was raising my voice. Even old closed-off me knew this was a sign of anger.

"See, some of the tension has gone out of your body because you're aware that I sense your anger. That's not hard, right?" He had me there. I nodded grudgingly and went back to writing an email to Mira's staff in Rio.

"I could teach you, you know. It would at least bring you closer to par with other vampires."

I slowed the key-pounding and looked at him. Was this a vampirish trick?

"No trick. I just thought you wouldn't be so ...so...touchy if you could read us better."

"I'm touchy?" My voice hit a note that Maria Callas would have envied.

"Ahhh, see? I knew that word would set you off."

He stood up, came around behind me and put his hands on my shoulders, running them up into my hair. His touch made the skin on the back of my neck shiver and little spasms of anticipation started down my spine.

"How can you say I'm closed off, when you just touching me makes my skin want to fall of my bones?"

He glimmered. He smiled. "That's sexual tension, a completely different thing. When I said closed off, I meant not able to read other people in normal communication. You're so used to giving orders that you don't allow yourself to see how that affects others. If you watch them carefully, you may see what they're actually thinking. Words are only one small form of communication. Open yourself up to others and it gives you a leg up when dealing with them. That's what I can teach you."

"Mmmmm, you can teach me anything right now." I stood and turned into his arms. He kissed me long and hard, then pushed me away. "Before you get nasty, this is only because I have a few more things I have to do tonight. Come and work beside me, I love having you near."

OK then, I could do this. I knew he wasn't going to go

away. I knew we'd make love tonight. Maybe not just right now. I went back to reading messages.

I suddenly realized that his hum, an almost inaudible small sound like a quiet purr he made when he was content, was gone and I couldn't sense his presence. I looked up. He was still here, he was just immobile, his eyes gazing at something I didn't see.

"Jean-Louis, my love, is everything all right?"

"Yes."

"What's happening? Why are you so silent?"

He shook himself as though someone walked over his grave. "I'm fine. I just need to go to Kiev. I'll be back soon." He stood up and headed for the door.

"Wait, wait, what's this 'I'm' going. I thought we were a team. And why do you, we, have to go?"

He was still watching events in Kiev, or where ever his attention was fastened. "I'm going alone. Nikoly is calling."

"And I just sit here, worried sick that you'll be killed while you boys go off on your adventures? I don't like this scenario. You said you wouldn't do this again."

Something in my tone...fear? desperation?...got through to him and he finally looked at me.

"You can't go, it's too dangerous."

"I don't care! I need to be with you, to know what you're facing. Please!" My pleading wasn't pretty, but he heard it.

"If you do come with me, there will be some very strict guidelines. I can't help Nik and look out for you at the same time."

Was he saying that I was going to be in the way? "I'll stay out of things, just so I know how you are. What's the matter with Nik?"

"It's not with him, it's what he's found out."

"What?"

"With you along, we'll have to take a plane, so you have 10 minutes to get ready. I'll meet you in the armory," and he was gone.

Oops, had my big mouth gotten me in hot water? How long would we be gone? Where would we stay? What should I pack?

Wait a minute! What difference would it make? I was going off with my vampire lover to help another vampire with a situation in the capital of Ukraine. It didn't make a whit of difference if I was wearing jeans or a color-coordinated pantsuit.

With the few working brain cells I could gather, I crammed a pair of jeans, a sweater, some underwear and bathroom stuff in a bag, grabbed another jacket and went out the door, right into Vladmir's chest.

He said, "Oof," I said "Sorry," and we barreled down the stairs.

Jean-Louis, Sandor and four other demons were loading up assorted weapons and ammo. In less that 10 minutes, we were piled into two limos and heading for the airport.

Demons moved fast, but these vampires could put on the speed when needed, too.

Chapter Thirty-three

Nik met the plane. Well, Nik, half-a-dozen demons, three limos and a vehicle that looked like urban SWAT transportation, were waiting when the plane taxied to a stop.

With Sandor, Vladmir, Vassily and two more of the Hungarian demons, we made a formidable force. At least *I* felt safe.

Pleasantries got short shrift as we sorted ourselves out and climbed into the various vehicles, Nik, Jean-Louis, me and Sandor in the middle limo. Ahead of us, three demons were the lead car and the third limo and the Urban Assault truck carried demons, guns, grenade launchers and an assortment of other weapons.

Our caravan seemed to provide the only light as we drove through the darkened Kiev streets toward Nik's house. I wondered why it was so dark, then realized it was after midnight. "Doesn't Kiev have street lighting?" I asked.

Nik and Jean-Louis exchanged as look. "Yes, but we took out a breaker on the way to the airport. This whole neighborhood is out. We and the demons can see perfectly in the dark; other Huszar pals, not so much."

"Who's causing the problem?"

"We know that Leonid has called in some reinforcements from around Kiev, but it's a little harder for their shapeshifters to work in urban areas, so we've heard they have the word out that they're hiring from some of the locals. And those are going to be regulars."

"They must have night-vision goggles," Jean-Louis said.

"They probably do," Nikoly agreed. "But even with night-vision, they won't be able to see as well as we do. So if we can keep most of the skirmishes in the dark, we're better off."

Once at Nik's we dumped our things and had a quick update. It seems that young women had been disappearing over the last few days and now the count was close to ten. That was bad enough, but there was blood spatter at the spots where each of the young women was last seen.

Plus, the police found a SNAP business card, with no name but a date penciled on the back, at one of the spots, in an alley behind a downtown club.

"A business card? That could have come from anywhere!" I was incredulous that it was even picked up, particularly close to a club. "It could have been there for days."

Jean-Louis closed his eyes. "Yes, it could have. From the police's perspective, though, it makes a strong assumption that someone from SNAP was somehow associated with the girl's disappearance. Maybe it was a legitimate appointment, and in that case, they'd want to talk to SNAP people as possible witnesses. A SNAP staffer could have been the last one to see her alive."

"You're right." Nik was pacing. "We've heard, though, that they're more likely looking for the SNAP person as the abductor. We have a couple of friends in the central police and they've been feeding us information. There's no particular person whom they suspect yet. Beginning tomorrow, they're planning to spend the day at the SNAP offices, interviewing everybody and taking fingerprints. Thank God they're not well-equipped or sophisticated enough for DNA."

He and Jean-Louis shared a laugh.

"What's so funny?"

"We don't really have a DNA profile. We have a lot of other people's blood running through us, so a profiling would just be complete mush." Jean-Louis smiled at me. "We have a wide variety of benefits."

"The problem is that the SNAP staff here are all regulars. They'll be absolutely panicked when the troops from Central come barging in tomorrow. We know who's been abducting young women—what we have to do is grab some of them and haul them into Central before SNAP gets completely shut down." Nik had succinctly outlined the problem. Now all we had to do was come up with a solution.

For the next hour or so, he and the Kiev demons laid out maps of the city and surrounding areas, plotting all the sites where a young woman had gone missing. Then they developed a grid for where these were in connection to Leonid's house and, surprise, surprise, they were all within a rough five-kilometer circle, with his house midpoint.

"How many Huszars are here?" Jean-Louis was looking grim. With the negotiations and work he'd done with Karoly, he'd hoped it wouldn't come down to a viscous and deadly stand-off with the family.

"Our sources say that three others have come to Kiev, plus five shapeshifters and who knows how many Chechens. The latest info we have, and this is from three hours ago, says they're all holed up at Leonid's. I think we have to attack tonight. If we don't, we're going to face a storm of criticism, bad press and an international black eye if word gets out about the business card."

Jean-Louis nodded at Nik. "You're right. This is a major problem that we have to solve tonight."

With Sandor speaking for the demons and me just listening, open-mouthed, Nik and Jean-Louis developed a straight forward assault attack. Two limos would pull up on the street behind Leonid's large home and six demons would go through the yard to secure the back doors. On their way, they'd also take out any guards Leonid had stationed, a job made easier by the black-out from the smashed breaker.

Nik and Jean-Louis would use another limo and come up to the front door. The rest of the demons would be in the Urban Assault vehicle, almost a tank, and be ready to ram the front of the house.

And me?

"Where should I be?"

Jean-Louis and Nik looked at each other. I could see that they'd forgotten about me.

"Uhhhh, I think..." Nik began. Jean-Louis took over. "You'll be with us. But when Nik and I go up to the door, you'll stay in the car with a demon."

"You're just going to walk in the front door?" That sounded like a kind of risky scheme to me.

"Well, yes. We're going to knock first. Depending on who answers the door, we'll either ask to talk to Leonid, push our way in or grab."

"Grab?"

"If Leonid or another of the Huszars answers the door, we'll grab him. He'll be a bargaining chip. Right now we don't have any. If it's a Chechen, we'll probably just shoot him. Same with a shapeshifter. Get him before he can change." Jean-Louis was matter-of-fact.

"If our information is right, there aren't any more than a dozen all together. That's an easy number." Nik was so excited he was all but licking his lips. Maybe this was one Kandesky who hadn't had all the hunter bred out over the centuries.

Jean-Louis noticed my startled expression. "Careful, Nik. Maxie's looking like she's going to make a break for it. She thinks you're on a hunting expedition!" They both snickered.

"It's true that we still have inherent urges to hunt prey. There's still a strong streak of that in regulars, too. We all come from the same original gene pool, so you shouldn't be surprised. The Huszars act on theirs, we don't, but it's there, under layers of civilization. Things like tonight's little party rip off the veneer, but we understand how to keep it controlled."

"Yes," Nik agreed. "To be honest, though, I still enjoy it. It's exciting, stirs up the adrenaline and sharpens senses. Right now, I'm hearing, seeing and smelling better than I usually do." He took a deep breath and his skin looked glowing, like he was pumping up for a marathon.

Even Jean-Louis was showing signs of excitement, and not the kind I liked. His eyes were almost black and were focused on something I couldn't see. Something I didn't want to see.

The demon driving turned off his headlights and we inched our way up a circular driveway to the front of Leonid's house. No outside lights were on, but windows on the first floor were lit by candles, judging by the flicker, and two windows on the second floor, maybe bedrooms, showed a low lamp light.

"Hmmmm...looks like they're up." Jean-Louis was tickled at his small joke. Of course they were; it was a house of vampires.

"I just hope they're not expecting us." Nik had put on surgeon's gloves and was coiling a woven silver rope. "I think we've moved too quickly for them to be prepared."

The car silently pulled up in front of the door.

"Stay here." Jean-Louis handed me a cell phone. "Keep this on speed dial. If things start to go bad, hit the button. There are another dozen demons on alert to come immediately."

He turned to the driver. "She is in your hands, and it means your life. Keep the engine running and be ready to leave instantly. Use the route we've planned, get to Nikoly's house and pull up all the barricades. Only accept calls from Nikoly, Sandor or myself. If you don't hear from one of us, call the pilot, get to the plane and get home."

Chapter Thirty-four

Jean-Louis and Nikoly were out of the car and at the front door before I could assimilate the orders he'd given the demon. Then it hit me—he was preparing for his capture or death. How could this happen? Weren't we stronger, better armed, better trained?

And what would I do if he died? I'd die myself.

I opened my mouth to say something, but what? Don't go? Be safe? I love you? Suddenly I heard his answer as clearly as if he'd spoken it in my ear, "I'll be safe. Remember I love you."

I whipped my head around, thinking he'd come back, but I could see he and Nik silhouetted in the open door. Then Nik's arm shot out, the candlelight gleamed on a streak of silver, a body was on the floor, Jean-Louis and Nik were in and the door slammed shut.

The night became dead silent. No traffic, no animal sounds. My eyes were adjusting to the full dark, but I still wasn't seeing anything. I jumped when a hand came over the back of the driver's seat.

"Take," the demon said. "Jean-Louis left for you." He was handing me what felt like a scuba mask. Why would Jean-Louis leave a scuba mask? I took the object and realized that it was night-vision goggles.

Bless you, my love. I wasn't up to being an actual participant in the battle, but these would let me know how it was progressing. I slipped them over my head and the world became an eerie greenish place, the lighted windows of the house so bright they hurt my eyes.

As I was getting used to the strange, new world, I caught a movement at the side of the house. It looked like a large dog, leaping over bushes and heading for the back. It disappeared around the corner into the back garden and suddenly I heard a long howl.

The demon in the car with me grunted in satisfaction and I realized that it had been a Huszar shapeshifter, a were, this one a wolf. I hoped the howl meant he'd run into one of our demons and lost the encounter.

The other action the howl meant was that four more shapes came across the garden, otherworldly large beasts who glowed green, with flashing red eyes. They streaked into the back garden and I heard low growls, soft ppffts, high-pitched yelps of pain and saw flashes of yellow-orange light. The sounds of battle wound down and two very large figures, black against the black night even with the goggles, crept around the corner and headed for the side door.

There was a brief flash of light that blinded me. When I could see again, the figures were gone.

"Went in house," the demon observer said. I glanced at him. No night-vision goggles, just tremendous night vision. Plus he'd probably been in battle lots of times and knew what to watch for.

"Shapeshifters gone. Now we wait." I trusted that he was right about the shapeshifters. They terrified me, huge wolves weighing upwards of 150 pounds, all bone and muscle whose only purpose was to hunt and kill. Between them and the feral pigs, it was a toss-up which was worse to meet at night in the forest.

The battle in the garden may have ended, but the one in the house was still raging. Figures were limned against the candlelight before they fell or were pushed through the windows. This time the guns weren't silenced and the continual fire told me that somebody was using full automatic weapons. There were grunts from the demons, keening shouts in a language I didn't recognize and abrupt explosions.

I looked at the demon for translation.

"We use weapons set on full auto, so do Chechens. Big

bang is grenades. Blowing down doors or wall maybe. Fire."

"I know they're firing, I don't know who the targets are."

"No, fire there," and he pointed at a window where flames were licking up an inside wall. Probably candles had been tipped over in the fight.

Oh God, somebody's going to report this! They'll call the fire department who'll bring the police and...and...I didn't know. At home they'd arrest everybody and haul them off, planning to sort it out later. Here, it was anybody's guess.

There were at least four bodies in the garden, shot with silver bullets from automatic weapons; automatic weapons and grenade fragments littered the inside of the house; there had to be five or six bodies on the ground floor and maybe other upstairs and, if Jean-Louis and Nik were right, the ten missing women. Who at this point were probably bodies as well.

I started to open the limo door when I heard Jean-Louis. "NO, stay where you are." I jumped, slammed the door shut and frantically looked for him. He wasn't there. I knew I'd heard his voice, though. Maybe it was my imagination. My first instinct was to go to him, but it was suicide to go into that burning house so I was imagining what he'd say to me.

The fire was working itself up the outside walls, the second floor was starting to burn and it wouldn't be long before the roof caught, taking the whole building with it. I certainly didn't need the night- vision goggles now, Leonid's burning house was lighting up the black night sky and must have been visible for several kilometers.

Against the flames, I could see figures moving around. An awful lot of figures. Maybe we hadn't inflicted as much damage as I first thought. The figures moved toward the back of the house and then the front door burst open, Jean-Louis and Nik flew out, slammed themselves into the limo, shouted "Now," and we peeled out.

I was beginning to get used to these demon drivers slinging me around and this time I smashed up against Jean-

Louis' chest. He gasped and it sounded like pain. I managed to back off and brace myself but I couldn't see anything, so I flipped on the interior light and gasped myself.

His chest was covered in blood, he had a gash across the top of his left cheek and his right hand, the one he was holding against he chest, was flaccid as though he had no bones.

I started to scream, but his good hand covered my mouth, stifling any sound. "Hush, it's not as bad as it looks." I heard his voice but I swear his mouth never moved.

He finally looked at me. "If you love me, please just stay silent. I need to get to Nikoly's, get cleaned up and start to heal before I'll be able to tell you what happened. Just know it's all right." He must have passed out. He was motionless and barely breathing, but it looked like the blood wasn't seeping out as fast.

I was horrified. In my limited experience, people with chest wounds like his were usually goners and if all the bones in his right hand were broken, he'd probably lose the use of it.

I wanted to cry. I wanted to scream. I wanted to throw up. I wanted to jump out of the car, find who or whatever had done this to this beautiful vampire and tear his head off.

I settled for a keening moan while hanging onto his left hand so tightly I'd probably break all the bones in that one, too.

Nik was having fast conversations on his cell with people and the demon wasn't saying anything, just driving at what felt to be a hundred miles an hour with the headlights off through deserted streets.

If this kept up, we'd all be toast.

Chapter Thirty-five

We wheeled through the gates at Nikoly's house, a demon ran to lift Jean-Louis out of the car and I tagged along, not able to keep up the pace but needing to be as close to Jean-Louis as possible.

He was carried upstairs and into a room equipped as well as some trauma rooms at home. Two other demons stripped his clothes off and began sponging the blood away and then I saw the full extent.

Jean-Louis had been shot in the chest, twice. The bleeding had stopped, but there were still ragged tears in his flesh. The doctor, who'd taken care of Nikoly before, came bustling in giving rapid orders in Hungarian, and the demons turned Jean-Louis over as I was protesting "Don't move him!". They started an IV with life-giving blood, brought in a portable X-ray machine for his hand and that was all I saw when Nik came in and led me out.

"But I want to stay with him." I cried. "I've never seen such awful wounds. Is he going to die? It that why you won't let me stay?"

"The way to best help him is to stay calm. Look at you, you're covered in as much blood as he is. Go get cleaned up, a maid will help you bathe, and then come back."

"He's going to die, isn't he? That's why you want me gone! It's the family, isn't it!"

If Nik hadn't been so polite, he would have slapped me to stop my blubbering hysterics. "No, he's not going to die! You don't understand how vampires heal. Get a hold of yourself, go do as I say. When you're clean and calmer, come back and we'll tell you what happened."

With Nik and the demons acting as gatekeepers for Jean-Louis, I didn't have much choice. One of the maids had set out my clean clothes, a shower was running and towels were warming. I caught a reflection of myself as I was getting in the shower and had a moment of panic. Nik was right, my face, hands and arms were covered with blood from where I'd been smashed into Jean-Louis' chest and then when I tried to told his hand.

I washed my hair twice and scrubbed with the bath sponge until I felt cleaner and calmer, then toweled off, dressed, ran a brush through my hair and twisted it, still wet, up with a clip. The entire ritual hadn't taken me more than 20 minutes and I tore down the hall to the trauma room.

He wasn't there. Two demons and a housemaid—masked, gloved and wearing scrubs—were cleaning up blood and dumping everything into biohazard bins.

I screamed and fainted.

I came to lying on a chaise in a dimly lit room. "Hello, feeling better?" Nik's voice was sardonic. "Jean-Louis says you over-react sometimes. I guess he's right. I told you he was fine." He motioned to a bed across the room from the chaise.

I stood slowly, not trusting my legs, and went over to find Jean-Louis, pale, bandaged and alive.

He looked up at me, his wonderful, expressive eyes now a deep violet shining in his almost translucent face. "My love." It was so soft it came out as a sigh. I didn't dare cry again. I knew I had to let him heal. "Tonight we'll talk. Nik and I will make sure we answer all your questions. For now, I need to rest."

"Of course. I'll do whatever you need to get well. I'm overwhelmed that you're alive. I love you." I leaned over and kissed his undamaged cheek.

He looked over to Nikoly. "Do you think you can find the doctor and get a Valium or something for Maxie? Knowing her, I suspect she'll be having bad dreams and may wake the whole house." He was able to manage a grin at me.

I'd been dismissed. Although I wanted to stay with him, be with him, the adrenaline was leaking out like air from a faulty balloon and I knew I was going to crash. Jean-Louis waved his good hand, a demon came in, picked me up and carried me off to my own room. One of the maids found an old t-shirt that I could use, I got a Valium and five minutes later I was gone.

I didn't remember much of what I dreamed. I did remember everything was red. When I opened my eyes, I was surprised to find that everything wasn't red, it was a washed-out gray, the color of a winter sunset.

Things were hazy. It was comfortable to lie there, starched sheets and duvet making a warm nest. I let my mind float until it finally landed on "Where am I?"

And with that, last night came rushing back. I threw my legs over the side of the bed, rummaged around until I found the cord for the drapes and looked out on a cloudy day sinking into sunset.

I'd slept all day. I found the lamp and checked the clock by the bed. It was almost 4 p.m. Time to take a shower, get dressed and plan for whatever the evening would bring.

In half-an-hour I opened the door to the hall and roused the demon standing guard. "I'm going to see Jean-Louis." He nodded, said something in his communicator and Sandor came out of a room further down the hall. I almost cried seeing a familiar face.

"How is he?"

There was no need to use a name, Sandor and I both had the same person in mind.

"He is healing. Come and have some coffee or tea. One of Nikoly's house demons will bring him up when he wakes."

"Where did he sleep? Did someone move him in his state? They could have made his wounds worse."

Sandor would have given an eye-roll if demons were capable of frustration. Instead, he said, "We have been caring for Kandeskys for many years. We would not hurt him," and led me down the room where Jean-Louis had been last night.

A bed was made up and coffee and tea pots sat on a credenza against one wall of the large room. Comfortable chairs flanked the bed, ready for conversation or stories. Sandor poured me a coffee and I sat by the bed, waiting for my love. And when he walked in I almost dropped my cup.

"What are you doing? You shouldn't be walking! You were on the verge of dying last night."

"And it's wonderful to see you, my love." He had a faint glimmer. "I'm going to rest on the bed while we chat. Nik will be along shortly."

I was stunned. Last night, or about 15 hours ago, this man was fighting off a close-to-fatal chest wound. Now he was standing, moving, breathing as though he'd never been shot. His right hand, so mangled that I thought all the bones were broken, was in a contraption that looked like a glove, blown up to keep his fingers straight. And the gash on his cheek? A slight red line held by butterfly bandages.

True, his skin still had a pallor, his eyes were surrounded by great, dark circles and he was moving more slowly than usual, but there was no resemblance to the dying man I'd left.

As he settled on the bed, he looked at me and a big grin split his face. "I really don't like being unwell, though if it keeps you quiet, I may use it again."

My fears of him being at death's door were instantly replaced with rage. "You rat! OK, tell me. Was that fake blood last night? What did you guys do, lay in a supply of movie props to scare to the women? How can you pull parlor tricks...?"

By this time he was laughing, just as Nik came in. "What's so funny? I wasn't sure I'd see you well enough to laugh yet."

"This one." Jean-Louis waved his good hand at me. "She's accusing us of using fake blood and parlor tricks last night. Do you think it's time we told her what really happened?"

Chapter Thirty-six

"It came off better than we'd hoped." Jean-Louis' eyes were half-closed as he recreated the scene. "One of the Huszars opened the door. He's now in the basement, waiting for us to kill him, which we won't do. We'll use him as a hostage."

Nik nodded. "Jean-Louis went left, I went right and we took out two more shapeshifters. There was a contingent of Chechens stationed at the back of the house and some of them opened up with automatic fire. For the life of me, I can't fathom why the Huszars didn't give them silver ammo, though. If they had, Jean-Louis would be gone now."

Thank god for stupidity!

"He got the worst of it. There were four Chechens barreling into that area of the house and Jean-Louis took two shots to the chest. It slowed him some, but our demons had breached a door by then."

Ah, that must have been the two large shapes I saw before being blinded by the light when they opened the side door.

"I must admit, those hits hurt. Maybe we should look into some body armor if this keeps up." Jean-Louis grimaced at the memory. "We've never had to fight like this. Usually just speed, agility and strength have been enough Kevlar wouldn't help against silver poisoning but if the Huszars hire from the gangs, the gangs might not think to ask for silver ammo. And I'm not even sure the Huszars tell them who the quarry is.

"For that matter, I wonder if the Chechens, Mafiosi, gangs or terrorists know who they're working for." He turned to Nikoly. "Let's make sure we ask the one downstairs, and do a little disinformation as well. We'll tell him that the Huszars never leave any traces of activities. All their 'employees' are used for food."

Nik smiled a smile I wouldn't want to be the object of. "That may cut down on their recruitment success."

"You're wandering off the subject. Was anyone still alive? Did any of our demons get hurt?"

"We didn't leave anyone alive in the house. We have one Chechen and one Huszar...oh, and Markov, downstairs."

Markov, where did I know that name from? I had it. Markov was a low-ranking Huszar who'd been recruited by Karoly and was one of the Huszar dissidents.

"I thought Markov was a member of Karoly's group. Did he go back to following Matthais?"

Nik shook his head. "We've been working closely here with him. He's one of those who tipped us to the probability the Huszars were behind the girls' disappearance. He gave us a detailed plan of Leonid's house so we didn't go in blind.

"And to repay him, he's the one we took to hold for ransom. That will strengthen his ties with Matthais."

Sandor tapped at the door. Jean-Louis said ,"Come" and the demon came in followed by two servants carrying trays.

"I know you haven't eaten since last night," he said to me, "and I need to take in a lot more to heal quickly. The IVs last night were wonderful, but my body is using energy at a fierce pace. Let's talk and eat."

He and Nik had borscht, steak tartre and Bull's Blood. I got a clear consommé, fish with a delicate lemon sauce and some vegetables. No alcohol, I just wanted water. Last night took more out of me than I realized.

Jean-Louis practically gulped his borscht then slowed down and sipped his Bulls' Blood. "We got separated with all the shooting. I could hear Nik yelling orders at the demons, then there were some grenade explosions. At this point, I didn't know who was dead or alive. I'd been hit with a piece of shrapnel and knew my face was bleeding. Nik finally yelled

'Here. Down here'. I followed his voice and found him and four demons at the head of stairs down to the basement. We flew down and there was another door, steel, guarded by a couple of Chechens who didn't last long. Before one died, though, he smashed my hand with his gun butt as I was reaching to put some plastique on the door."

"Jean-Louis has to get every lick in." Nik's words were kidding and his tone was reverence and love. These men had been friends, family, comrades-in-arms for many. many years and the affection between them was clear.

"Once the door blew off, we saw that the girls, the young women, had been packed into a small room. There were sets of bunk beds, a single toilet, it looked like a prison cell."

"Were the women alive?" I was imaging the abject fear and terror they must have felt. I'm not claustrophobic, but being in some place, trapped, with no way to tell where I was gave me the frights.

Both men nodded. "They were alive. That's about all they were." Jean-Louis closed his eyes.

"They'd been drugged," Nik said. "We don't know with what. A couple of them had marks, bites, on their necks so they'd been food for the Huszars. We don't think they've been turned yet, but we're keeping an eye on them."

"Keeping an eye on them? Where are they?"

Jean-Louis smiled as Nik said, "You were out of it last night. Just as well, you didn't see or hear anything. It keeps you innocent if there's any blowback.

"When Jean-Louis and I came out the door of Leonid's, the demons were carrying the girls out the back. They loaded them into the assault vehicle—and I'm glad we didn't have to use it any more than that—and brought them here."

"They're here?"

Nik looked please with himself. "Yes, we have them safe and comfortable in a couple of guest houses. They've been checked over by the doctor. No permanent effects, other than a few marks that will fade quickly."

"But how can you have them here? Won't they be found? Won't they tell everyone what happened?"

"No, no one will ever know. We've given them a drug that produces selective amnesia. They'll remember who they are, they'll remember their families and they'll have all their memories intact right up to when they were grabbed."

It sounded like a plausible and sensible plan, until I remembered the inferno.

"What about Leonid's house? It was lighting up the whole neighborhood when we left. Surely someone saw that fire and called the authorities."

Boys and their adventures. Jean-Louis smiled. "Well, we lit it and we certainly hoped someone called. That was a big part of our plan. When the firefighters got there, they found the remains of a huge battle between two rival gangs. There were bodies on the grounds, naked and with no identification. We know they were weres. The Ukrainian cops think they were stripped by the Chechens so they couldn't be ID'd.

"Inside the house, the bodies were badly burned, but one of them was identified as a Chechen chief through tattoos. Voila! A shootout that meant a bunch of gangsters had gotten rid of each other. Everybody's happy."

There were just a couple of points I didn't understand.

"What about Leonid? It's his house. Was he killed?"

"Oddly enough, he went out of town earlier that day. One of his servants confessed that he was being blackmailed by the Chechens and forced to let them use Leonid's house for a high-level parlay. Their rivals, probably Russian Mafiosi, got wind of it and laid on an ambush. Which, as we know, went horribly wrong." Jean-Louis could hardly contain his glee.

I turned to Nik. "You're the one who has to live here. Won't there be repercussions? Won't Leonid be after you?"

"Probably not much more than before. He's been recalled by Matthais and I'm sure is getting a stern talking to. When he gets back, he'll be more vigilant but less likely to try something so public again. The Chechens are royally pissed, I imagine, losing so many of their own. Plus having this fight plastered all over the media."

"The media! I forgot all about the SNAP business card."

"Hmmmmm. Somebody called the SNAP Bureau Chief, Taras, while the firefight was going on and a crew from SNAP was right behind the firefighters at the scene. If SNAP is remembered in this whole thing, it's more likely to be as the media that broke the story."

Chapter Thirty-seven

It seemed like Nik and Jean-Louis had handily managed everything. I wrote a mental note not to cross them.

A maid came in quietly to remove the remains of dinner. Jean-Louis was looking better and better. I knew that food and rest were the best remedies for healing but with him, I could almost watch the tissues regrowing and bones knitting.

How did he do that?

He and Nik exchanged a look again and then he smiled at me lazily, like a cat curling up before a fire. "I told you we had benefits."

"You did it again! You read my thought. That makes me crazy. OK, as long as we're there, how do you do that."

"I told you, practice patience, keep yourself open to all forms of communication..."

"No, that that! The healing. I can practically see the cells replicating and you getting stronger. That mark on your face. When you came in tonight, it was a red line, now it's disappeared. Nobody heals that fast. "

The two vampires all but giggled.

"What's so funny? I asked you a perfectly civil question."

Jean-Louis tried to put a sober expression on and failed. "It's always such a treat to see a regular when they witness this for the first time. We're not exactly sure how it happens. It just does. We think it has to do with getting nutrients through blood, it allows cells to reproduce quickly. And this." He held up his right hand and I could see that the bruising was gone and the swelling decreased. "I think that by tomorrow or the next day, the bones will be healed."

My mind was swimming. Last night I thought he might die. And I was sure that he'd lost all use of his hand. Tonight, he had almost no trace of his horrendous injuries.

"I told you we have benefits. We can come back to them again, if you still have questions."

Did I have questions? Lord yes, I'd always have questions about this vampire and his life. I was so confused and astounded that most times I couldn't even articulate what I wanted to know. He *was* an onion. And every time I peeled off a layer, a new one popped up. I'd never get to the core and I wasn't sure I even wanted to. Part of the allure, the overwhelming charm of this man was his unknowingness, his constant surprises and his otherness.

"Yes, I can come back to them. For now, what's going to happen next?"

"If you mean with the Huszars, we're going home and call a war council. The Baron and I, Nik, Francois, Bela, Milos, Pen, Carola, a few more. Maybe it's time that Stefan and I talked about Felix and what we know. Our plan of assimilation with the dissidents isn't moving fast enough to keep us out of these skirmishes."

"I agree." Nik headed toward the door. "These are just part of a war of attrition, trying to wear us down. We need to take a position of offense, bring this home to Matthais. I'm going down to make sure our guests are ready to leave. The girls will be taken to spots close to their homes. They'll be found, safe, with no memory of what happened to them. Makov and the other Huszar will get shipped to Hungary tonight. As soon as Jean-Louis gets home, he'll arrange for talks of reparation."

When the door closed on Nik's back, Jean-Louis reached out and stroked my face. "The other thing that's going to happen next is that I'm going to make love to you for a long, long time. Right now, that's the best healing tool I can think of."

As he traced his fingers down my neck and over my breast, I quivered. "Oh my love, I was so afraid I'd lost you."

"You haven't and you won't. Come lie next to me and let me show you how well I'm healing."

I took care pulling his shirt off and stared at his chest. Last night there were two gaping wounds where the Chechen's bullets had hit. Tonight there were two red, indented spots. I touched one. "Does that hurt?"

"No, not hurt. It's tender, like I imagine a bruise would be on you."

"I tried to tell them not to move you last night but they flipped you over on your stomach. That can't have been good for you. Do you know why they did that?"

He smiled at me. "I love that you were trying to protect me. It's standard to look at the back, to see if there are exit wounds. It's good if there are, it means the bullets passed through. They wouldn't have to poke around inside looking for one."

I was resting my head on his chest and lifted up to ask him something that never got said. Instead, his mouth came down on mine so hard it took my breath away. Then my body responded. My mouth fell open to try and absorb all the hunger and desire that was in his kiss, I wrapped my arms around him and he rolled me over on my back. He broke off the kiss, pulled up to look at me and I felt a tremor run through his body.

He nestled his head between my breasts and began kissing me as he worked his way down my body. This time, the tremor was mine and I couldn't stop it until we both collapsed.

What seemed like hours later, I finally got my thoughts to coalesce around what I wanted to ask.

"You keep telling me that you can't read minds, that it's all careful observations and recognition of body language. But I've seen you and Nik. You communicate with each other and you both seem to know what's on my mind, even when I try to keep still."

His voice said, "I know". His mouth never moved. Now this was freaky. I knew he had some telekenetic communication skills.

"See, you just did it! And at Leonid's house, I started to go find you when all the shooting started and your voice said 'Stay', but you weren't around."

This time he looked at me and smiled. "You're right. I wanted to wait to tell, or maybe show, you this. As a regular, your mind was closed to much of our knowledge. You wouldn't have understood, or been able to manage our techniques. Now, you've been around us, me, enough to see and learn some things. That command at Leonid's house was a test. If you'd gone ahead and started toward the house, the demon had orders to pick you up and restrain you."

"Why didn't you just tell me? "

"It's not all of a piece. When I talked to you about observation, I meant it. We don't have the ability to just speak to people in our heads. There are certain levels of telekentic communication that we have with certain people and certain types of people. Within the family, we can read, or better is 'see', the other's thoughts when emotions are concerned. We put what we see internally together with what we observe through sight, and understand what the other is saying or feeling."

I sat up and wrapped part of the duvet around me. He never felt the cold as much as I did.

"What about other people? Regulars?"

He pulled me and duvet down to lie against his shoulder. "We don't bother trying to read regulars beyond observation. They, you, live in a loud and noisy world where most information comes through hearing. You've developed bells and whistles and sirens to tell one another to be careful or to announce danger. We use some of those as well. We also use silent warnings, silent commands. Not only does it keep our physical presence unknown, we can communicate over much longer distances."

He paused to pull me closer. "It's easier to just take regulars at their level, far less confusing."

"Can you teach me? I'm not sure I want to read *your*

mind, but I'd like a way to keep some of my thoughts private. Even from you."

An odd expression flitted across his face, then, "Yes, I can do that. There are two sides to this. One is to be able to understand what someone else is thinking and the other is to shield your mind from showing what you're thinking. That's a little harder for regulars, because they give so much away in other ways, like body language."

Suddenly, I was overcome with exhaustion. The drain of the adrenaline that had kept me alert—actually hyper-alert—for the last 30 hours left me wrung out. Jean-Louis noticed, although it may have been the enormous yawn while he was talking that tipped him off. A demon came in, probably called by Jean-Louis' non-ability to send nonverbal messages, Jean-Louis asked him to carry me to my room and I was out of there and in my own bed before I could yawn again.

No medication tonight, I was unconscious before the door closed.

Chapter Thirty-eight

We put the tutorial on hold until we got back to the Baron's and then, of course, there were a myriad of details to get the war council together. Getting many of the senior editors of SNAP to leave their offices and gather in Hungary on a moment's notice was iffy. Schedules were rearranged, planes were readied, demons were called back home.

I had a day to myself and used it to take a long walk around this place that I was calling home.

With two weeks to go until winter, and almost to the Christmas season, activities were ramping up. Our coverage of holiday parties, the minor royal wedding, frantic shopping, kept all of our staff and free-lancers busy.

And the vampires were busy and euphoric, too. After the winter solstice, the days would incrementally grow longer, so this run-up was a heady time for them as well. Villagers were often seen at the castle in the long evenings, chatting with Stefan and Pen, giving Jean-Louis hearty handshakes and exchanging small tokens, usually a piece of jewelry.

The grounds around the castle were headed for hibernation. We'd had one night of snow and the trees looked stark against the gunmetal gray sky and the pristine snowy ground. Firs still held some snow on their branches, glistening like Christmas trees when hit with a ray of sun.

I didn't know the name of the demon who escorted – guarded?—me, but I was taking them more for granted now and not bothered by the anonymity. The air was cold against my nose and throat and burned the tips of my ears, but I relished it.

Jean-Louis had opened me up to sensations and sensual pleasures. This walk in the cold, still air, knowing that warmth, big fires and hot drinks were going to follow, brought tears because of the enormous simplicity of it.

How odd to be taught to live in the now by someone with eternal life. Maybe if we lacked a knowledge of death and the finite length of our regular lives, we could let go of the frenetic pace of how we lived.

When the demon and I came in through the armory, stomping the snow from our boots and with me clapping my hands together to jumpstart circulation, Sandor was there taking inventory.

"Elise has been waiting for you. She said you need to get ready for dinner."

I didn't bristle, I didn't snap. Sandor was just the messenger. A few days ago I may have been annoyed at being given an order, but now I was absorbing the text and subtext and beginning to weed out my instant emotions.

A hot shower warmed my outside, a hot brandy warmed my inside and I was ready to go when Jean-Louis tapped on the door and came in.

"You look lovely. Is that a new dress? It suits you."

He had ceased to surprise me with his observations of small things. I was slowly understanding that he vacuumed his surroundings, taking in all that was there, using the relevant and discarding the rest.

"Thanks, yes. Jazz had it sent from Saks. That personal shopper is almost always spot-on. I've only sent two things back."

This particular choice was winter-white soft wool, high-necked but sleeveless with a drapy golden belt that hung on my hips. It hit the curves in the right places, but was loose enough to allow easy movement.

"What's the agenda for tonight? Will we have some time for ourselves?"

He gathered me up in his arms and licked my earlobe. "Yes, we'll have time."

I sucked my breath in and moved back from him. "Not

for that, well, yes for that, but I meant for my next lesson in mind-reading."

"Aahh...I do wish you wouldn't call it that." He was miffed, not really angry. "You make it sound like some carney side-show attraction. 'Come into my tent and let me read your mind for only $1.' That's not what this is about."

After a moment of silence, "Yes, we'll have some time for that, and for this." He leaned over and kissed me, hard. "Let's go, now."

And we went.

Tonight, there were twenty-seven for dinner. I was stunned to see the table stretched to accommodate everyone, but the sheer size made it difficult to talk with anyone beyond immediate neighbors. Stefan was at one end, with Pen on his right, and Jean-Louis was at the other, with me at his right, a bold statement for those who weren't privy to our relationship. Many of the family, for these were all members, knew that Jean-Louis and I were a number, but this announced that I was trusted and permanent.

Gatherings like this showed off the castle and the Kandeskys to their best. Although there was wi-fi in every room and satellite communications, flat-screens and smart phones, a closet full of servers and firewalls as good as the National Security Agency, tonight the huge dining room was lit by a massive fireplace and a rank of candelabras marching down the table.

The flickering light prismed off cut crystal that was red with Bull's Blood and reflected pools of crimson on the white linen. My consommé, chicken vol-au-vente and salad paled on the bone china in comparison to borscht and steak tartre.

With dinner over, the crowd moved into the screening room and arranged themselves around a massive conference table. The screen was pulled down and what looked like piles of corporate reports had been dealt out to each place. Stefan and Jean-Louis took their seats in front of the screen and the war council of the Kandesky vampires began.

"As many of you know, I've just returned from Kiev," Jean-Louis began. "Nikoly called for help with a problem he assumed was Huszar related. When we got there, we found that Nik was right."

Nikoly, seated along one side of the table, stood. "We'd heard rumors that not only had the Huszars teamed up with the Chechen again, as when they tried to grab Maxie in Paris, but they'd gone a step further. They'd begun abducting young women from around the Kiev area. They were planning to turn some of them to use as bait for SNAP coverage. The Chechens could keep the others, probably to sell as sex slaves. Our demons and I followed their movement for a few days and we were convinced that Leonid had the girls stashed in his house."

Jean-Louis took up the narrative. "Nik was right, we found ten young women kept as prisoners in Leonid's basement. Three of them had recent bites on their necks, so the turning process had begun. The Chechens were dropping hints and forensic clues that SNAP was involved in the kidnappings and this had to stop immediately."

The room lights dimmed and video of the fight at Leonid's house was thrown up on the screen. "As you can see," Nik pointed out areas in the house, "even before the fire there was severe damage. Once we started the fire, there wasn't enough left to conduct any forensic testing and besides, why bother? The entire episode was written off to gang rivalry, supported by the stripped bodies on the grounds."

Stefan stepped up to the head of the table. "We've called this council together to figure out how best to stop these predations once and for all. These are skirmishes, but if we have to fight enough of them, we'll be unprepared when a true battle breaks out.

"I'm announcing that the Kandeskys have to go on the offensive and declare war."

There was silence. This was a family of vampires who had spent the last several hundred years peacefully counting their money and living well, if quietly. They'd all killed at some point and understood the necessity of it, especially on a one-to-one basis with a rogue Huszar. And they all had pride of family. A full war, though? This was not a comfortable idea.

Francois stood. "I'm aware of their techniques. I was supposed to be with Maxie when she was attacked in Paris. I agree these have to stop, but isn't there some way of negotiating a truce? We're brighter, have more money, have more position..."

"Yes," another vampire broke in, another whom I didn't know. "Why do we have to fight these 15th century idiots on their terms? Why can't we bring them to ours?"

A chorus of voices broke out, pushing for a negotiated peace rather than all-out war. Jean-Louis let it run its course and when the room was quiet again, said "Let me tell you what we've been doing."

Chapter Thirty-nine

For close to an hour, Jean-Louis, Stefan and occasionally Nik went over all the attempts they'd made to bring revolution to the Huszar leadership. Without naming names, they talked about the clandestine meetings held at the castle, the lengths they'd gone to disguise any Huszar involvement, the disinformation they'd fed back to Matthais.

When they finished, Chaz stood up. "Like many of the others, I had no idea it was this desperate. I have the luxury of being isolated from the family's day-to-day problems in L.A. but I want to go on record as supporting whatever Stefan and Jean-Louis chose to do. I'm behind you 100 percent and will help in any way I can."

At this, everybody chimed in, a couple of the younger vamps even banging emphatically on the table which earned them the fish-eye from Pen.

Stefan then stood and waited for silence. "I thank you all. As you know, unlike our neighbors, we have been careful and selective in our acquisition of acolytes. This now is bearing fruit. We do and will present a united front." He turned to Jean-Louis. "Bring them in."

Jean-Louis picked up a communicator, said "Now" and Sandor opened the door to escort Markov, Karoly and Alessandr in. Both the Kandeskys and the Huszars were silenced, and wary about being in the same room with age-old rivals. One Kandesky began a low hiss and was instantly quieted by a look from Stefan.

"Tonight, we meet for one purpose. To design a method of bringing this vicious and stupid tension to a close. A short time after I was turned, another vampire appeared. His name was Felix . I was settling into the area where I finally built the castle and Felix wandered over a large area, feeding and indiscriminately turning peasants. After about fifty years, he had a large band of followers, while Pen and I had started our family with twenty-two carefully selected acolytes, among them Jean-Louis, Milos, Bela and Nikoly. As Felix' family grew, they ranged over a larger and larger area, until we were running into each other every time we went hunting."

One of the Kandeskys I didn't know had a frown on his face. "You're too new to the family. You became an acolyte after we'd given up hunting and foraging for food," the Baron told him. Then he turned to the full room. "I know there are several who don't remember the old days. That's why I'm going back."

"We had to do something if both our families were to survive. We, the Kandeskys, were beginning to branch out to trade, moving more into the regulars' world, so we began experimenting with food to see if we could live without hunting and killing. It was during this time that Felix and I developed the Neutrality, a swath of the forest where we agreed to never hunt."

The Baron's story continued, taking the group through almost three hundred years of growth, consolidation and pact-building. As the Kandesky's moved into trade and fanned out to all the mercantile centers of Europe, Felix led the Huszars in the direction of controlling large areas of small and isolated villages, developing a form of agriculture.

This lasted until Felix turned a young man named Matthais. Matthais was ambitions, ruthless and a consummate plotter who quickly worked his way up to second in command of the Huszars. Felix doted on him, pouring on him all the affection he would have given a son.

Just before the turn of the 20th century, it was obvious to all that tensions were rising in Germany and the Austro-Hungarian empire, the area of Central and Eastern Europe where the Huszars hunted and cultivated their prey.

"We heard rumors that Matthais was stirring up dissent. It didn't much matter to us, we were too busy making money and expanding to the Americas." The Baron paused, his expression turned inward as he relived the past. "Then, they began to flaunt forays into the Neutrality. This was land we'd agreed to keep in trust and they violated it. We sent many peace emissaries and negotiating teams to Felix. He listened and agreed, but it was clear he was losing control over Matthais. The Neutrality raids continued and we fought back, losing two of our family members and a few demons."

The lights were still dim from the video presentation, making the vampires' eyes huge and dark. I glanced at Jean-Louis and a twinge of fear went through me. If I hadn't known, trusted and loved him, his look would have sent me running in terror. These vampires may have been worldly, sophisticated, urbane, but they were vampires. It was like looking at your pet dog and suddenly seeing the wolf inside him.

The moment passed. Jean-Louis took up the story. "One day, we assigned a watch patrol for the Neutrality. Two Kandeskys and two demons. They were moving quietly, using silent communication, when they heard noise—snarls, shrieks, hisses. They crept up to the spot and watched as a band of Huszars attacked someone. After using silver rope to immobilize their prey, we watched them stake two figures to the ground then leave.

"When it quieted down, we went over to the assassination site—it was an assassination—and found Felix and a companion, dead."

There was no sound in the darkened room. Everyone was stunned to silence at the story of greed, murder and usurpation.

Stefan's voice was tightly controlled as he told how emissaries from the Kandeskys went to the Huszars, looking for explanation. What they found was Matthais taking absolute control over the family, banishing dissenters into the edge of their territory and to the small, isolated villages of Eastern Europe.

"Eventually, we found out that Matthais was blaming us for Felix' death. Our presence in the Neutrality that day had been noted by shapeshifters prowling through the woods. We suspect that the entire scenario was staged, with 'witnesses' to convince the rest of the family that Matthais couldn't help Felix and barely escaped himself." Stefan stopped.

"That's where we are today." Jean-Louis broke the silence. "We have more than a century of lies, deceit, murder and violence we now have to set right. We've been leaving them alone, thinking that their hatred wouldn't harm us but a couple of things have happened.

"First, the end of the Cold War and the opening up of the former Soviet states. This brought immense pots of money to the region, and we're moving to corral some of it. That frosts Matthais. Not only do we have wealth in the rest of the world, but now we're moving in to what has been their exclusive hunting area.

"Then we brought in Maxie to oversee our expansion. They don't have anyone who can compete with her, so if they want to keep their territory, they need to stop us from moving in. That means they need to turn Maxie. With her as a Huszar, they'll have the ability to stop us. And, eventually, they plan to take over our entire business."

Now it was my turn to be silent.

I don't think I'd actually thought this whole thing through. And Jean-Louis being coy about giving me information hadn't helped. So, that ass, that killer, that crud, that jerk wanted to turn me!

I think not!

If I wouldn't let the one I love near my neck, I for sure wasn't going to let some backwoods cretin get a lick.

Chapter Forty

The meeting resolved into committees willing to take on tasks. Chaz would chair the committee for propaganda, putting out rumors, statements and press releases about our push into Eastern Europe and our stunning successes. Maybe even small hints about the fat bottom line we expect.

Nik's committee would fan out along the new border areas, probing for soft links, those Huszars tired of Matthais' haranguing and bullying

Jean-Louis would work with Karoly and Markov to get Matthais' Big Lie counteracted by the truth.

And Bela and Milos would start amassing weapons and ammo, placing a lot of smaller order for silver bullets and rope. Even though the Kandeskys owned the armament factories, there were Huszar spies around and a huge order would cause speculation.

And me?

Jean-Louis leaned over and softly said, "Are you ready to learn?"

At least I think he said it. I whirled around to look at him and he wore his I-wouldn't-lie-to-you face. That usually meant he was stretching the truth. Maybe I just heard his words in my mind. I mouthed, "yes" and we headed upstairs.

Once in my apartment, I wound my arms around his neck. When I pulled his head down, I met resistance. "What's wrong, don't you want to kiss me?" Even though I was learning to control my impatience, my voice was petulant.

"You are such a ninny sometimes! I despair that I'll ever see you be a grown-up." He was glimmering, so he wasn't angry. "We have to work on getting your mind to cleanse itself and shut off probes, but at the same time be open to learn new things. It's a balancing act."

"Hmmmm. If I'm going to school, I'd better be comfortable." I kicked off my shoes, pulled the dress over my head and went into my closet for one of his shirts.

He laughed. "Why, with all the clothes you have, do you wear my old shirts? They're much too big for you, you have to roll up the sleeves, they can't be comfortable!"

I tried for a Cheshire cat smile. "Oh, but they are. The material is soft, they're roomy enough to wrap around my knees and they always have your scent. When I wear one, it's as though I have you with me all the time."

That actually shut him up.

"Whatever," he said, flinging his jacket over a chair and rolling up his own sleeves.

Whatever? A lot of the mannerisms of these formal vamps were rubbing off on me, but it felt good to see that he was taking on some of me, as well.

We sat across from each other in front of the fireplace and his great violet-black eyes bored into mine. I felt myself slipping into some nether world, where I only had sensation, no physical body. Then I heard and felt, "This is what I'll teach you. How to eliminate all the extraneous signals and focus only on the truth, the communication between two minds."

I'd never felt words before, but his were bathing every part of me, pulling me closer and closer into his mind.

Then I snapped out of it. "What did you do? I was being drawn closer and closer to you."

"Yes, I know. I didn't want you to go into a trance, and I didn't want you part of my mind. Not now, not yet. I was only trying to show you what could be done."

"So you hypnotize people? *That's* your silent communication?"

He grimaced. "This is going to be harder than I thought. You have such a shell. Have you ever studied yoga?"

I nodded. "I took yoga classes for exercise in L.A."

"Well, that's a baby step, but a step. What I'm going to teach you is a form of mind...control...maybe mind relaxation. The closest regular activity I can think to describe it is the practice of yoga. And I don't mean the Beverley Hills Saturday morning variety before a tennis lesson and tanning session. Can you will your mind to go blank?"

I gave him a blank stare. "I don't know. I've never tried."

"Think about us making love. Think about the times when you're solely sensation, you have no conscious thoughts. That's the state you need to be in to send and receive messages."

"I can't do that! I can't be in a constant state of arousal! Besides, that's only because of you..." My voice trailed off as I became aware of him in my mind saying "Hush, hush, I'm not talking about the sexual part."

He began having me concentrate on things in the room, the fire, the drapes, the sofas, to the exclusion of all else. As the night wore on, I began to absorb his voice as I felt the sensation of being part of the objects around us.

In the early hours, he stopped. "You're beginning to understand. Now I'm going to give you sensations to remember until tonight," and he stripped off his shirt I was wearing, laid me in front of the dying fire and started making love to me.

He was right, I was only sensation, even as I woke in the afternoon. When Elise tapped on the bedroom door and brought in coffee, I jerked back to my conscious reality. I didn't remember going to bed—or maybe being put to bed by Jean-Louis—but I had a hazy memory of talking with him most of the night.

"Are you working today?" Elise pulled the drapes apart to a winter sun, making the leaves drip and the runoff soak the ground. "I think now the small animals feel safe coming out. The pigs don't wander too far when it's muddy. When the freeze starts, they'll be back."

I showered, pulled on some slacks and a sweater and

tackled the backed-up emails. The usual, but Jazz was doing a superb job of balancing all the bureaus and facilitating the feeds to the TV show. I'd have to talk to Jean-Louis about giving her a generous year-end bonus. The pay scales at SNAP were about the best in the business, but an extra few thousand at Christmas wasn't frowned at.

The castle was oddly quiet for having close to thirty additional people in attendance. The local Kandeskys, Bela, Milos and the others, would have gone home to sleep, leaving Chaz, Nikoly, Francois, Mira and more, with assorted demons, as houseguests. The vampires were still asleep., but I expected Josef and Lisbet, the supervisors of all the regular house staff, would be bustling, setting tables, readying fires and laying in supplies. Cooking—well, preparing—food for the Kandeskys was dead easy, nonetheless, it had to be ordered and served.

I went down to the armory to pick up a jacket and a demon, and here there was some activity. Sandor was supervising three demons who were unpacking and storing boxes of ammunition and keeping a running tally of all the weapons.

"Do you feel we're prepared, Sandor?" I asked more for form's sake. I didn't really want to think about what was coming.

He gave me a long look. "Yes, we can handle it all," he said and turned to his laptop.

Ooooo. Was he being disrespectful? Maybe he was blaming me for bringing the wrath of the Huszars down on his beloved Kandeskys. I'd have to talk to Jean-Louis about this, as well.

The sun was for show and not substance. It was colder than I suspected and a quarter of an hour was enough. The demon, I'd given up keeping the visitors straight, didn't show any reaction, except to hold the door for me. All in all, not very satisfactory exercise.

There were fewer at dinner this night. Francois, Nik, Chaz and Mira left for home to get their projects underway. The locals, including Bela and Milos, ate quickly and excused themselves to meet with Sandor and a contingent of demons.

The chat was subdued and after dinner we watched both the US and French editions of SNAP, jotting down notes and criticisms. but nobody seemed to put their heart into it.

By midnight clumps of two and three were talking quietly. Jean-Louis stood up, took my hand and led me upstairs.

"That was preemptory of you. Did you forget how to speak?"

He looked at me as he opened the door. "That was a test. And you failed."

"I failed? How did I fail?"

"I said we need to get started on your practice. Time is running out. Apparently, you didn't hear me."

I hadn't heard him. My mind was idling along, not paying much attention to anything, jumping from thought to thought. All he'd taught me last night about concentration had flown the very leaky coop that was my brain.

He grinned. "Usually your mind isn't a leaky coop. What's changed?"

"I don't know. All day hasn't felt right. There isn't enough of the present present .to get a hold of," and I told him about Sandor's comment.

"He wasn't being disrespectful. Demons are never that. He must have sensed your discontent."

"Am I that transparent?"

"Yes, you are. We need to work hard now to change that. We worked last night on accepting your surroundings. Tonight, we have to master shielding yourself, your thoughts. There may be danger and that's the only way you'll survive."

"Danger? What danger?"

He leaned against the mantel. "You want to be with me. You don't want me to go off, making you wait behind. As a regular, the only way you can be with me is if you're protected. It's for your safety and ours. Kiev was a test to see if you could be open enough to receive. You heard me, and you acted sensibly."

I remembered hearing his voice and I remembered absorbing the items last night. Apparently, I had been learning, but wasn't retaining.

"I told you what I was teaching you was like regulars and yoga. When you were doing it, did it just come naturally after the first lesson?"

"Of course not. You have to practice it to get...oh."

My work was cut out for me. I had assumed that his ability to know, his ability to see what was in my mind, was inherent, like having ESP or being color-blind. He was telling me that it was acquired and had to be studied and practiced. Just one little wrinkle here. He'd had close to 500 years to perfect it. I was trying to cram it into a couple of nights.

"You're beginning to see. Now let me tell you the last piece of it. We're planning a raid in two nights. Our target is Matthais. We aren't going to kill him, because then he would just become a martyr and our troubles would multiply. We're going to bring him to justice. We're setting up a trial, inviting all the Huszars who care to come, to expose his perfidy."

Kidnap Matthais? Put him on trial? It was a risky undertaking that would pay off with a jackpot if they could pull it off.

"Where do I fit in?"

"If you're ready, if you want, I'm inviting you along with the raiding party."

Chapter Forty-one

Oh. My. God. He was asking me if I wanted to break into the Huszars' fortress and kidnap the head of the nasty family, the vampire who had brought misery to the countryside, the vampire who had supported Hitler because it served his ends, the vampire who was trying to wipe the Kandeskys off the face of the earth.

Well, maybe not.

Of course I wanted to go. I'd be with Jean-Louis. I'd get to meet this horror who was bent on destroying my home, my family, my love.

And, truth to tell, I was scared witless.

I had a mouthful of "what ifs" when he put a finger across my lips, then leaned over to kiss me, gently, gently.

"I know you're frightened. And you should be. Even a lot of us are scared this might not go well, but we've hedged our bets. The faction led by Karoly is growing and he's arranged for many of them to be recalled home for a planning session. Maybe ten percent of the Huszars at the castle the night of the raid will be ours."

That made me feel better. Still terrified, though.

"What do I have to do?"

"You have to practice to proficiency your ability to close off your mind. We aren't the only ones who have silent communication. Once they spot us, the Huszars will be probing for any way to get into our minds."

"And what if they do?"

"This attempt will fail. They'll learn we're going to put Matthais on public trial. And we think this is our best, last chance to rid ourselves, and the Huszars, of this aberration, this Stalin, this despot."

So I practiced and practiced and practiced. Cleansing my mind of all my memories, putting up a wall of nothingness. When Jean-Louis looked into my mind, he needed to see that I was only focused on the now. He could see my apartment, sense it through me. He could see the things I saw, smell the things I smelled, but not feel the things I felt.

For the next two nights, he pushed me to practice, practice and practice some more. He tested me by communicating verbally and non-verbally. He had Sandor or other demons, burst into the room. He had Elise serve coffee and ask about my clothes. I wavered once. She asked me what I wanted to wear to a house party the Baron was planning. I let my mind wander over my wardrobe and Jean-Louis was on it in an instant.

"Hah! You've just given me entry into your thoughts! It's like hacking a computer. Once I learn the way your mind makes decisions, I can trace that to your recent memories. And once that happens, our entire strategy is open. You have to keep the wall up."

It was the hardest mental effort I'd ever put out. Way worse than cramming for finals. Way worse than memorizing channel schedules in 25 different countries. Those were efforts at stuffing facts in. This was an exercise in covering facts up. It wasn't a case of wiping the hard drive clean, I'd need to have all my memories and all my knowledge when this was over. I didn't see how Jean-Louis was able to switch back and forth. Probably the same way he thought and spoke in several languages without having to translate in his head. He trained himself to compartmentalize his mind.

And then, something clicked. I had a room in my mind. When I went in that room, all I saw and heard and felt was the now, like watching through a lens. I stayed in that room until I opened the door and walked out, out to where all of me, my life, my memories, my feelings, lived.

Jean-Louis watched my face as I concentrated on going

in and out of the room. "I can see you understand now. I think you're ready."

I closed my eyes and was in my room, with fingers of mist and fog trailing around the outside walls. They weren't a distraction, I didn't see them or feel them, but I had a awareness they were there. When I opened my eyes, Jean-Louis's glimmer intensified.

"You passed well. I sent probes. You had no reaction. Well done, love."

High praise!

Mind-work wasn't my only task to get ready for the raid. I spent hours with Sandor, shooting various weapons until I was able to hit the head and chest of the target. He gave me my own .22 handgun, loaded with silver bullets, two extra magazines and fitted me for a Kevlar vest.

"You wont' be able to kill anyone with this unless you're on top of them, but if you hit a Huszar, the silver will slow them down and give us a chance to get to you," the demon gave me a look that could be affection.

"Thank you for teaching me, Sandor." My voice was raspy with emotion.

Jean-Louis noticed that. "Sandor, I thank you. You've touched her with your caring and warmed me with you concern. I value you, old friend."

Sandor bowed his head. "Sir, Magda was taken from you. I could not stop that. But Maxie will not be taken."

Ahhh, another piece fell into place. I knew that these two went back, but had no idea that the demon felt any responsibility or remorse for Magda's death. Now the constant, cloying closeness of the demons was clear.

And it was also clear that the demons assumed I was Magda's replacement. A frisson of fear mixed with joy ran up my back. Jean-Louis loved me, considered me as permanent as any regular could be, and yet was willing to let me be part of a risky scheme because he knew I needed to be with him. This was monumental.

We, Jean-Louis, Nik, Bela, Milos and myself, gathered for a fast meal before the raid. This was a hurried meal eaten while Jean-Louis was pacing. "Stefan, are you ready to receive our visitor?"

"The basement room is set. We've replaced the steel door with silver bars. He'll be confined to a space only big enough to lie down. I thought about silver chains, but we need him able to stand trial. I don't want him to show up in the dock with silver poisoning."

All of us in the raiding party headed for the armory where we picked up our weapons, body armor and a contingent of demons. It was 5 a.m., the raid timed to be completed just before sunrise. Jean-Louis wasn't taking a chance that either the Kandeskys or Matthais would be caught outside when daylight hit.

The door to the tunnel swung open, Sandor took the lead and we headed into the earth to bring Matthais to justice.

Chapter Forty-two

This time, I had night-vision goggles. They didn't want any sound, any light, to escape to alert the night animals, let alone any roving band of Huszars, shapeshifters or other sentinels.

Our journey was silent, thanks to Jean-Louis' order that everything—weapons, magazines, communicators, silver handcuffs and rope—was Velcroed to our clothes. The vampires wore surgical gloves to guard against silver poisoning and the demons and I wore thin, flexible black ones. Against the dark night, we would be less than deeper black shadows, sensed rather than seen.

At the end of the tunnel, one of the demons lifted me and flew up the ladder with me. In an instant, our raiding party was assembled at the edge of Huszar territory in the Neutrality.

The green glow of the goggles showed stands of virgin trees, the forest before regulars had logged it or used it for fuel. On the floor of the forest, paths and trails led through the bushy growth, lanes that patrols used for reconnaissance and the feral pigs used for hunting.

Jean-Louis said, "We'll take the left one." I stared at him, then realized he'd sent the message, not spoken it. I'd passed one test.

We moved out at a fast pace, me being practically towed along in the slipstream of the lead demons. The forest whizzed by in a faint green blur. So far, there hadn't been any living animal show up, but a sudden flash between trees resolved itself into an owl, grabbing a vole and making off with it. If I hadn't had the goggles, the quick breeze from his passing wouldn't have registered.

We were at the Huszar castle? house? compound?

before we ran across our first shapeshifter, a wolf. A soft pffft and he was down, dissolving into a one of the heavy-shouldered Slavs the Huszars kept around.

I had a brief glance at the compound. One main building, stone, three stories high judging from the glow of candles at windows small enough to be arrow slits. Dating maybe to the 17th century. It was flanked by two smaller wings, also stone, with no windows. Dormitories for the help? Bedrooms for the Huzsar vampires?

A separate, newer building sprawled in front of the left wing. This one must be the office complex, with a couple of satellite dishes on the roof. And this one had windows. A glance blinded me. The lights were on and someone was home.

Low voices behind me. I heard Jean-Louis. "It's Karoly. He'll lead us in."

Spoken? No, it was silent again then Jean-Louis. "Can you see us?"

I sent back, "Yes" when I found a few green blips. Vampires didn't show up on night-goggles as clearly as other warm-blooded animals, their outlines were hazy but I could locate them easily.

"Follow us and make sure you have demons." The blips disappeared through a door in the main building and I followed them in.

The inside of the Huszar stronghold *was* from the 16th century. Massive furniture lined the walls of the main room. A dying fire in the huge fireplace threw out flickers of light, showing tapestries maybe ten feet tall hung for warmth against the bare stone walls.

But even with the fire, the tapestries, some rugs on the floor, it was cold. And clammy. I'd become used to the Baron's castle, a bastion of warmth, light and comfort, even beyond what the Kandeskys needed for themselves. Stefan, Pen, Jean-Louis and the rest of them had moved gracefully into the regular world of the 21st century. All the tales I'd heard didn't prepare me for the medieval world where the Huszars lived.

I took the goggles off. The room regained dim colors and I saw Karoly and Jean-Louis in one corner talking furiously. In my head, Nik's voice said, "Matthais is in his quarters, getting ready for sleep. Markov, Alessandr and Karoly will take us to him. Bohdan and some others are in the sleeping area. Most of the Huszars take a small drink of blood from a supply they keep on hand just before going to rest. We've put drugs into that."

That sounded like a plan. I wondered who he was talking to.

"You. Stay behind us." OK, that was Jean-Louis.

I sidled over to the corner, swiveling my head around, looking out for any movement. All I heard was a low chuckle in my ear. "Most of them are immobilized. Let's go."

This parade was led by Karoly, followed by Jean-Louis, Nik, Sandor, me flanked by two demons, and several more demons doing a Secret Service tail—whipping their heads to take in 360 degrees, maintaining a constant low chatter on their communicators and earbuds. We sped down a long, dank hallway lit by flaring sconces and pulled up at a door guarded by Markov. He nodded, stepped back, a string of pffts echoed from the stones and the heavy wooden door swung in. Here was Matthais, feeding off a young dark-haired woman while another sat beside him on the bed, waiting her turn.

My anger was rising, my heart was pounding and Jean-Louis was in my head. "Be careful, be careful. Don't let him sense your blood!"

I willed myself still and clinically looked over this creature who would destroy my life and happiness.

Matthais was a beautiful man and I understood Felix' attraction and felt how he maintained his power.

He was blond, his hair combed back from a high, white forehead. His dark, soulful, bedroom eyes, looked out sleepily from a pale, almost delicate face. As he raised his head to see what caused the intrusion, a drop of bright red blood oozed its way down his chin. He lazily licked it up with a long tongue as the young woman moaned, "Please, please."

Then all hell broke loose. Matthais threw the dark woman to the floor, began hissing and whipping around the room looking for an exit. Jean-Louis executed a cowboy noose toss with his silver wire and caught Matthais' arm as he pulled himself back for another pass.

He slowly sank to the floor as the silver sapped his power until he lay at Jean-Louis' feet.

"Get up." This time Jean-Louis spoke. "Don't think we're going to drag you out. You'll walk out of here like a man, not the scum you are."

The dark woman snuffled as she pulled herself up and slid over to her companion, a blonde whose eyes were enormous in her ashen face. "What are you doing with Matthais? Who are you ? Please don't hurt us." The blonde was gibbering in fear, although I'm not sure what was scarier than being sucked on by a vampire.

"We're Kandeskys, and we're arresting Matthais for the murder of Felix." Jean-Louis looked and sounded judicial, an avenger come to right a wrong.

That was in the eye of the beholder, though.

"You're crazier than that old Baron you hang with." Matthais' voice was weakened by the silver but his hatred was strong. "What makes you think I killed Felix? And how are you going to prove it?"

Jean-Louis' face was carved marble, a Biblical prophet fashioned by Michelangelo, stern, angry and implacable. "We have witnesses."

"Who cares about your supposed witnesses," Matthais hissed. "You don't frighten me. What do you think will happen when you kill me? I have legions of followers who will hunt you and yours down for all eternity. The Kandesky name will no longer exist and all that you have will be dust!"

"Stop spouting that nonsense." Now it was Jean-Louis' turn. "What makes you think we're gong to kill you, although it would certainly stop all that neo-classical babble or whatever you're throwing out. Have you been reading the

Christian Bible? Looking for good curses?"

This time, Matthais's hiss climbed to a shrill screech and Jean-Louis looped the wire around his neck, shutting him up until a demon could wrap duct tape over his mouth.

Duct tape? I'd seen the silverish roll but didn't put it together with the best-loved, most-used method of getting someone immobile and quiet.

"No, Matthais, we're not going to kill you. We're taking you to the castle. You're going to stand trial and we're inviting as many of your followers who want to come. A safe-passage will be offered to all. You'll be our guest for a few days until we get all set up."

He turned to the two women huddled at the edge of the bed. "Please dress yourselves and our demons will conduct you to your home."

"This is our home," the blonde said. "Matthais promised us that he would make us famous. He is going to get us contracts with SNAP in return for us being donors to him."

Jean-Louis and Nik looked at each other and I could hear their confusion about this. "For now, get dressed. We'll take you back to the Baron's castle and figure things out from there." He turned to me. "Maxie, help them pull themselves together, then tape their hands behind them. They'll have to get carried by demons."

I threw clothes at them, then pulled their hands behind, taped them tight, ran a piece of tape across their mouths and handed them off to two demons. I was learning new skills by the minute. If SNAP fired me, I could always go into kidnapping.

Meanwhile, Nik and Jean-Louis held Matthais as Sandor wrapped a sheet around him and then pulled a net of thin silver wire over that. They wanted him still, but not silver-poisoned. He'd have to appear unharmed when he faced his trial.

When we were ready, demons hoisted Matthais and the two women, Nik opened the door, Markov gave an all-clear and we sped back down the corridor. I looked back just as Jean-Louis was stabbing Markov in the arm. Why? He was an ally.

"This will keep him safe." Jean-Louis in my head. "He'll have a mild case of silver poisoning, he'll recover, and his bravery will convince the Huszars that he tried to save Matthais."

Jean-Louis took the lead of our convoy and we burst out the front door just as Markov sounded the alarm. Lights flipped on in the office complex and we heard doors slamming open in the dormitory wing, but by the time Huszars or their shapeshifters emerged, we were well into the forest and headed for the Neutrality. The vampires were speeding full-tilt, the demons not loaded down were firing on automatic, bullets were plowing into trees and occasionally something else, which grunted. A pig, a shapeshifter, a Huszar?

I was pulled along by the demons, but I'd lost my goggles somewhere in Matthais' so I just ran, blinded, where the demons led.

Jean-Louis was shouting, "Here, here, the tunnel is here" in my head but there was no direction for his voice. I stopped for a second to look for the steps, heard a soft grunt behind me and was suddenly flying through the trees. I closed my eyes, unable to see a thing and hoped that whoever had me had night-sight.

We slowed, I opened my eyes expecting to see the Baron's castle, and looked at Matthais' compound. I screamed, was dumped on the ground and found myself facing terror.

Leonid hissed at me. "Did you and your pals seriously think you could pull this off? I'd love to suck you dry, to turn you, to make you my slave, but that's for later. I haven't forgotten the snubs and attacks in Kiev. For now, your life and well-being is in the hands of Jean-Louis. How you fare will depend on how Matthais is treated. You'd best talk to your lover!"

My lover was screaming in my head, and I screamed back, "Leonid has me!"

The last words I heard from Jean-Louis were, "Go to your room! Stay there! We'll come! Stay in your room!"

My mind bolted into my safe room, where only the present lived, and I began an exile from all I loved.

Excerpt

The Kandesky Vampire Chronicles
Book Three, Plague: A Love Story

Prologue

Another Scourge of God swept across the barren Asian steppes to consume Europe in the middle of the 14th century. It didn't come on horseback and couldn't be seen. This outbreak of the Black Death killed more than a quarter of the population. No one knew where it came from. No one knew what caused it. This was the time when the killers were out.

Panic set in on such a scale that the Christian nations of Europe witnessed parades of flagellants, traveling from town to town, lashing themselves and praying for intervention.

This first wave hit in 1347 and four years later had burned itself out, taking 25 million souls with it. But that was just the first. Almost every subsequent generation saw smaller waves, killing hundreds of thousands more.

When plague hit, people fled to the countryside, moving out of the miasma of filth and overcrowding in the cities.

In this disruption of civil and family life, some things thrived.

Other killers were at large in the forests, definitely in the woods that climbed the slopes of the Carpathian Mountains. This was a wild place with high upthrusts and deep ravines, cold streams and thick, untamed woodlands.

A few trade routes wound through these foothills, and

even fewer led to the crags that pierced the sky. Small villages dotted the little arable land between the hills and a scattering of families braved the woods to eke out a living by cutting timber and burning charcoal. No matter what these people did during the day to feed and clothe themselves, at nightfall all were inside, huddled with their animals behind locked and barred doors. The peasants were at risk from both inside and out and the vampires reigned the dark hours.

*****

He moved the pack to the other shoulder. It wasn't heavy, only enough flour, some salt, to keep him alive for the next three months. Winter already dusted the higher peaks with snow. The secluded valleys held a faint remnant of the summer's warmth, now pallid, a mockery of the sun that brought heat and growing weather.

After Lisle and the child died, he didn't need much.

He looked up from the path, seeing the sun sink behind the forest on the ridge. He had to hurry if he were to make it home before dark. It wasn't only himself he was worried about. No one was left of his family, but he still had the animals—a pig, a cow, two goats—to bring in and feed. And the chickens. Without these and the flour he carried from the mill, three miles down the river in the valley, he'd starve to death this winter.

He had no plans for the future. Every day would be like every other day, filled with simple chores so that he and the animals would live through the winter.

Dusk came rapidly and a small moon lit the path as night robbed the earth of color. He went more slowly now, afraid a misstep would lead him into the forest. He could just hear the cow, lowing to be fed, but there was another sound as well.

Rustling of leaves? Swoosh of wings? He turned to look for an owl and was thrown to the ground. A voice said, "Don't fight it. It will be over soon," he felt a searing pain in his neck and then nothing.

Made in the USA
Charleston, SC
17 November 2014